DEATH
and the
COURTESAN

PAMELA CHRISTIE

KENSINGTON BOOKS
www.kensingtonbooks.com

KENSINGTON BOOKS are published by

Kensington Publishing Corp.
119 West 40th Street
New York, NY 10018

All Kensington titles, imprints, and distributed lines are available at special quantity discounts for bulk purchases for sales promotion, premiums, fund-raising, and educational or institutional use.

Special book excerpts or customized printings can also be created to fit specific needs. For details, write or phone the office of the Kensington Special Sales Manager: Kensington Publishing Corp., 119 West 40th Street, New York, NY 10018. Attn. Special Sales Department. Phone: 1-800-221-2647.

Kensington and the K logo Reg. U.S. Pat. & TM Off.

ISBN-13: 978-0-7582-8640-6
ISBN-10: 0-7582-8640-6
First Kensington Trade Paperback Printing: June 2013

eISBN-13: 978-0-7582-8641-3
eISBN-10: 0-7582-8641-4
First Kensington Electronic Edition: June 2013

10 9 8 7 6 5 4 3 2 1

Printed in the United States of America

Acknowledgments

For their unflagging assistance during the writing of this book, the author wishes to thank the following persons:

Jacob Greenleaf and Vanessa Pepoy, for feeding me when I was hungry, for letting me sit in front of their fire when I was cold, for listening while I read the entire book to them and for laughing at the parts that were supposed to be funny.

Meg Cristofalo, for her reassurance and rosy predictions.

Dr. Thomas Biddison, for listening while I read the second half of the book to him in the car during a single trip from Los Angeles to Cambria and for his general support, encouragement, and excitement over the whole thing.

Michele Rubin and Brianne Johnson at Writers House, who believed in the book, promoted it, and got it sold.

And Philip Randolph, for suggesting that Arabella should keep a pencil behind her ear.

DEATH
and the
COURTESAN

Chapter 1

ON THE COMPARATIVE MERITS OF
BUILDING MATERIALS

*In which Constables Hacker and Dysart
have their work cut out for them.*

"Decent people what's only tryin' to make a honest livin' oughtn't to have to put up wi' this sort a thing. I've ast 'er nicely, I've ast 'er firmly, an' I've threatened 'er wi' the law, but the hussy looks right through me as if I was made of glass!"

Though the heavily built landlady appeared to have been formed of *some* type of construction material, it definitely wasn't glass, and the two Bow Street Runners who followed in her wake exchanged smirks as she led them up the dark staircase. Visibility was poor in here, and the steps were strewn with objects both lumpish and sinister, but neither constable was inclined to grasp that handrail a second time.

"Oh, she was nice enough . . . to begin with, first tellin' me I'd be paid in full . . . by the end o' the week, then in a fortnight . . . then by the end of the month . . . Said she 'ad expectations from somewhere . . . but either she never got the . . . money, or she spent it all . . . soon as it come in."

The landlady paused on the landing to catch her breath.

"Have you got the key with you, Mrs. Ealing?" asked one of the constables.

"Yes, lor' bless you, sir! I remembered it this time!" She

produced a key from her pocket, and the three of them trudged down a narrow passage that reeked of cat. " 'Ere we are: number five." She pounded on the door. "Open up!" shouted Mrs. Ealing. "I've got the law with me, you baggage! They've come to throw you out on the street! Do you hear me?" She rattled the knob, but there was no sound from within. "I know she's in there. Prob'ly dead drunk. It's a disgrace, is what it is!"

Mrs. Ealing unlocked the door, which swung open before her into the room. But she remained standing where she was, like a wall in her own right, blocking the entrance with her bulk, and the officers had to push past her in their haste to reach the ghastly thing that lay upon the bed.

Walls are typically made of stone, or brick, or wattle and daub. The good ones can be counted on to maintain perpendicularity for years. But the landlady swayed and toppled after only a few moments. Not a bit like glass. Nor stone, for the matter of that. Mrs. Ealing, at this moment, resembled nothing so much as a pile of wet cement.

Chapter 2

SUSPECTED!

*In which Arabella suffers a change of plans,
the duke recalls a previous engagement,
and Lady Ribbonhat writes a letter.*

The morning on which Arabella was served with a warrant for her arrest dawned like many another summer's day in Brompton Park: brimming with birdsong and sunshine, punctuated with gently rustling leaves. For it was June, glorious June, and London the most lighthearted of cities, if one happened to be rich. There were no dark clouds, no eerily howling dogs, no unaccountable feelings of foreboding. Nor was there any sign of the duke, other than a checque for five hundred pounds that he'd left beneath her pillow. But this, too, was typical.

Arabella smiled and stretched herself, as the accustomed light tapping at her door heralded the appearance of the chambermaid, bearing Arabella's breakfast. She was in an excellent humor.

"Good morning, Doyle!" said Arabella, pulling herself upright to receive the tray. "We leave for Bath in two weeks! Are you excited?"

"Oh, yes indeed, madam! Cook's been tellin' us ever so much about it—'Tis like the way our mam used to talk o' London, when us were little and hadn't ever been here!"

"And did London live up to your expectations?" asked Arabella, tucking a crisp linen napkin into her décolletage.

"In some ways. In others I can't say as it has, ma'am."

"Well, I think you'll find Bath very satisfactory in all particulars, Doyle. It is the one destination which never disappoints." She lifted the cover from her plate. "Oooh! Enormous, masculine sausages! I *do* love those!"

The maid tittered. It suited her, too, for she was a tiny thing, and Irish. "If you please, ma'am, His Grace the Duke is waiting to see you downstairs."

"What? Isn't he gone, then?"

"No, ma'am. That is, he *was* gone, but he's come back again, and says for you to please take your time; he'll wait in the library until you want him."

"Want him . . . ? Why should I? Well, thank you, Doyle. Tell him I'll come down when I'm dressed."

Arabella poured a rich, steaming stream from her silver chocolate pot into a delicate pink cup with a golden rim. How odd; why should the duke think she wanted to see him? She'd already seen him—quite a lot of him—over the past three nights. And hadn't he mentioned something about attending a breakfast meeting at his club?

She took a bite of toast and picked up the paper. More news from the front. Napoleon had . . . blah, blah, blah. And Wellington was nearly . . . oh, blah blah . . . war was *so* dull. And yet people scarcely spoke of anything else these days. Surely, there was something in the paper besides politics. . . .

Oh! Dear! Now this was too bad! Euphemia Ramsey was dead! Murdered night before last! She and Arabella had once been friends, but they'd fallen out some years ago. It was more than just a falling-out, actually; they'd become enemies. But nobody deserved to be murdered. Not even Euphemia.

Hmm, stabbed to death with a paper knife . . . Dear, dear! Suspect's arrest imminent . . . that was good. Owner's initials engraved on handle . . .

Arabella stopped chewing and sat very still. A week ago, after one of her parties, a silver paper knife with her initials had gone missing. Oh, but it couldn't be that one ... could it ... ?

She thrust aside the tray and hurried to her dressing room, where she selected a rust-colored muslin frock with dark-green ribbons, and dressed quickly. Then she swept up her hair with tortoiseshell combs and dabbed her eyes with orange-water from the basin under the window. There was no time to do more, nor was there need: She was looking her best this morning, in spite of, or perhaps owing to, the fright she had just experienced.

Now we shall pause, reader, to take stock of the celebrated Arabella Beaumont, England's most famous courtesan. She was handsome, rather than pretty, but she made the most of everything she had, for, as Arabella herself was famously quoted as saying, "There is no limit to the heights attainable by a passably attractive, intelligent woman, knowledgeable in the ways of pleasing men, and entirely free from inhibitions." The gray-green eyes were narrow and long, the full lips shapely, and she nearly always wore, not so much for ornament as for use, a stub of pencil behind her right ear. Upon meeting her for the first time, one had immediate and simultaneous impressions of height, abundant auburn hair, and a Grecian profile—the bridge of the nose dropping almost straight down from the forehead. There was nothing the least bit childlike about her looks, and the sort of man who prefers the infantile innocence of helpless little maids would not have pronounced her beautiful, perhaps; yet even such a one as he should have found it difficult to resist her graceful elegance and engagingly direct manner of speaking.

Arabella's protector, on the other hand, was conventionally good-looking. So there can be nothing more to say about his appearance. The eye of the beholder slides off countenances such as these, there being no single feature to fix upon or excite interest, and Arabella used to quite forget what he looked like when they were separated for more than a fortnight.

When she entered her library, the duke set down his pen and rose from the writing desk, opening his arms.

"My poor darling!" he murmured, kissing her brow. (For Arabella was tall, but the duke was six-three.) "Such a sorry business!"

"I don't believe it, Henry!" she cried. "Surely there has been some mistake!"

"I am afraid not, my dove; I spoke to Sidmouth this morning. He's serving a warrant for your arrest today."

"But they can't really think *I* did it, Puddles! I've been here with you the past three nights! The servants will swear to our being together!"

The duke took her hands and gazed earnestly into her face. "I am afraid we shall have to keep that to ourselves, Bell. I didn't like to tell you before, but you see . . . I'm . . . getting married soon, and my fiancée thinks . . . well, she thinks I gave you up six months ago."

Arabella abruptly withdrew her hands.

"I'd no idea you had a fiancée, Henry!" she said coldly. "There's been nothing about your engagement in *The Times*!"

"We haven't told anyone. Her father always thought me a despicable roué."

"And so you are, darling. Who is she?"

"Doesn't matter. But the paterfamilias finally popped off last week, and she's a very wealthy woman now. Not that I need it, but money's a good thing, and more money is even better. Besides, my mother is dead keen on the match. So I can't . . . You see?"

"What?" cried Arabella. "Not even if they hang me for a crime I haven't committed?"

"Oh, they won't, Bell. I've told Stinker off the record where I've been spending these past few nights."

"And who is 'Stinker'?"

"Old Sidmouth's son. We were at school together."

"Well, that's some help, I suppose. Still, without your evidence I might very well hang. If I don't rot in prison, first."

They had moved into the entrance hall and were standing next to the front door when it suddenly commenced pounding.

"Open up in the name of the law!"

The flustered parlor maid ran in from the passage.

"Oh, madam; whatever shall I do?"

"Open the door, Fielding," replied Arabella calmly. "It's the law, you know."

The two blue-coated constables who stood outside appeared abashed at finding themselves face-to-face with a London celebrity. They stood, shifting their weight uneasily, and shyly removed their hats.

" 'Ave I the honor of addressin' Arabella Beaumont?" asked the fair one.

"You have, sir," said she. "Won't you come in?"

The two officers stepped carefully over the threshold, conscientiously wiping their boots on the mat.

"I'm very sorry, miss, but I must read you this warrant."

"That's quite all right, Constable. You may proceed."

The warrant was read and the officers were on the point of escorting her out of the house when the duke, who had heretofore remained in the background, stepped forward at last.

"One moment, if you please."

"And who might you be, sir?"

"I am Henry Honeywood Seaholme, the Duke of Glendeen. I have here a letter, written by myself and addressed to Lord Sidmouth, the home secretary, promising to guarantee

Miss Beaumont's continuing presence in this city until the time of her trial, and requesting that her person be remanded to my custody and protection for the remainder of this month. Naturally, I shall be happy to pay whatever security is required."

He handed the letter to the dark-haired officer.

"Well, Your Grace, I don't know if—"

"It's quite all right, Constable. Lord Sidmouth advised me to follow this procedure himself."

"Oh. Well. That's all right then, I suppose," said he, glancing uncertainly at his partner. "We're sorry to have troubled you, Miss Beaumont." He gave an awkward little bow and murmured, "I'm a great admirer of yours, ma'am."

"Not at all, Constable," she replied graciously. "You were only discharging your duty."

As they were leaving, Arabella partially closed the front door and put her head through the opening, where the duke couldn't hear her. "And I hope," she added softly, "that you will both pay me an *unofficial* visit when all this is cleared up." For they were strong, good-looking fellows!

After she had shut the door, the officers stood perfectly still for a moment. They looked at each other and swiftly looked away. Then the fair one reached up, firmly grasped a tree branch, and swung from it, uttering a single, curiously ape-like cry. His companion, dipping his hat into the bird-bath, poured water over his own head and gasped like a landed fish.

Meanwhile, on the other side of the door, Arabella had turned to the duke.

"Why did you say 'for the remainder of this month'?"

"Well, because that's when my leave ends, you know."

"And do you really expect them to have this matter resolved by then?"

"Um, well, probably, yes. I sail for Lisbon on the twenty-ninth."

"Where will I be, then?"

"Well . . . here, I suppose. I mean, if they solve the murder, you'll be free and everything."

"But, Henry, what if they *haven't* solved it?"

"Um . . ." He couldn't meet her eye.

"I shall go to prison, shan't I? And then they'll hang me, while you're off in Iberia." She slumped against her benefactor. "Now I can't go to Bath, and I did *so* want to meet Jane Austen! That is, not *meet* her, of course, but have her pointed out to me in a shop, or something."

"Who is Jane Austen?" he asked, walking her back to the library with his arm around her.

"A terribly clever new writer, who's known to frequent that place. No one is supposed to know her identity, but I am friends with her publisher. I shouldn't imagine you've heard of her." They sat down upon the sofa, holding hands. "Didn't you say that you have an awful lot of idle time on your ship? I could lend you my copy of *Sense and Sensibility,* if you like."

"What's it about?"

"Two sisters and their search for love."

"Hmm. Is it a dirty book?"

"Rather the opposite."

"Well. Doesn't sound my sort of thing, you know. I mostly confine my reading to manly subjects of a salty nature, like sea battles and pornography. My men wouldn't half laugh if I should be discovered with dainty literature in my quarters."

Arabella sighed. "The servants and I were so looking forward to Bath," she said. "Oh, Puddles, what am I to do?"

"Why, nothing, my dear! I'll get you Corydon-Figge!"

And he attempted to ease her onto the floor, with her head between his knees.

"I really don't feel up to eating, Henry."

"You mistake me, my darling!" said the duke, fumbling with his breeches. "I meant Sir *Clifton* Corydon-Figge; the best barrister money can buy!"

Arabella pulled sharply away from him and stood up.

"And you mistake *me*," she said, shifting the emphasis of the words in order to clarify her meaning: "I meant I really don't feel up to eating *Henry*."

Lady Ribbonhat was taking longer than usual over her correspondence this morning. She would scratch a few lines and then sit quite still for extended periods, staring vacantly at the wallpaper. One could hardly blame her, for she had recently had the morning room re-papered in an ostentatious gold foil, at great expense, and staring at it was one way—really the only way—that she would ever realize her money's worth. Even so, some might have thought the walls better suited to a typically pompous dinner with the regent than a lovely summer morning all to oneself. Framed silhouettes of Lady Ribbonhat's favorite pugs hung above the desk on pink satin ribbons, and sometimes she stared at these, rather than at the wallpaper. But neither her golden walls nor the pink and black pictures adhered thereto reflected the duchess's mood today, which roiled along like an angry river, in deepest, bloody purple. For her heart was overflowing with anticipated vengeance, which her head had determined was almost at hand. She was writing a letter to Arabella, and considering the venom that coursed so forcefully through Lady Ribbonhat's veins at that moment, the reader might find it curious that she should experience difficulty in getting it to flow from her pen. But the explanation is a simple one: In such matters it is of the utmost importance to strike exactly the right note, and poor Lady Ribbonhat was somewhat tone-deaf.

At length, however, she was able to produce an epistle that satisfied her requirements well enough:

Madam,

I am to be rid of you at last! As you have no doubt been informed, my son has made a good match, and, concerning his relations with you, his future wife has quite properly forbidden him further intercourse, of either type. I have therefore taken it upon myself to communicate the following:

1. That your tenancy at Lustings cease immediately.

2. That your belongings be removed from the premises by Monday next.

3. That any articles remaining after that date shall be thrown into the street, or become the property of the new owner, your rights to said articles having become null and void.

This can hardly matter to you, in your present circumstances. If, however, you should find yourself in need of lodging before they take you out and hang you for a lawless baggage, I am certain that I can have my son's protection revoked, and a small but ever-so-cozy prison cell provided for you.

Yours &c.
Lady Honoria Gwendolyn Ribbonhat, Viscountess Mintly and Duchess of Glendeen

Lady Ribbonhat seldom used her full title, since everyone to whom she wrote knew perfectly well who she was, and it took too long to write out. But the dowager wished to strike fear and awe into the breast of her enemy, and like a vulture with its talons out, sought to improve her chances of success by descending from a greater height.

This paragon was the possessor of a large head and a runty body, shriveled with the years. A pair of pale eyes with pendant lids sat too closely on either side of a high-bridged, beaky nose, beneath a heavy pair of crow-black eyebrows. The hair upon her head, however, was the color of mayonnaise.

Rightly ascertaining that the new fashions were too young for her—just now they were modeled on the gowns of the ancient Greeks, and, as Beau Brummel had once famously observed, Lady Ribbonhat was at least as old as the pyramids—she remained more or less loyal to the styles of her own day. Full crinolines and corsets and buckle shoes were much in evidence, but she no longer affected the white lead makeup, nor the high powdered wigs that had always made it so difficult to get in and out of coaches. As a matter of fact, Lady Ribbonhat was thoroughly au courant in her choice of headgear, which, coupled with her complete lack of taste in gowns and accessories, created effects of startling originality.

She would not have dreamt of communicating with our heroine on a social level. Nevertheless, the older woman was obliged frequently to think of her, for the trollop had taken control of her only son, Henry. What if he should marry her! Well, he wouldn't now, of course; she had managed at last to match him up with Miss van Diggle, but it had been a near thing, probably. No, Miss Beaumont would never become a duchess now, and Henry had promised not to see her again, but she still had the house he had given her. And Lustings was rightfully Lady Ribbonhat's. Why, it had been built for one of her own husband's ancestors' in-laws! And she herself had always intended to spend her declining years there. She *still* intended to do so, for Lady Ribbonhat was a stickler for rules and, like many sticklers before her, knew how to bend them to her own best advantage. Had she not been too grand for nicknames, some wit would doubtless have dubbed her "Lady Loophole."

Now that Arabella had lost her protector, the path to Lust-ings would be easier, but it was the fact that Miss Beaumont was also in imminent danger of arrest that had decided Lady Ribbonhat upon her current course of action. For, whereas common decency admonishes us against kicking a man whilst he's down, there is no corresponding social code pertaining to women.

Chapter 3

THE OMNISCIENCE OF SERVANTS

*In which Arabella says good-bye to her house
and Belinda rinses her mouth out.*

Dear Charles,

I write to you, dear brother, in much
distress, having been accused of murdering
Euphemia Ramsey. Than which, as you know,
nothing could be sillier, as I have always been and
am still a calm and rational woman, and not
given to sudden outbursts of passion, excepting
only in the intimate matters that pass between a
man and a woman, and indeed, not always then.

I am vouchsafed my liberty at present, owing
to the intercession of His Grace the Duke. But
probably, in fact almost certainly, I shall be
incarcerated at the end of this month, when
Glendeen sails to Sicily, or wherever he is going,
and his clemency expires. Then I expect to be tried
and hanged, the prosecution having at present no
other suspects than myself. For of course, they
must hang somebody, mustn't they, and I
shouldn't be surprised if you are already giving
odds on my execution date.

Therefore, I have updated my will,

arranging for you and Belinda to receive small but sufficient annuities. Only in your case, Charles dear, you will have to collect said amounts from the bank each month, as you and I both know what you would do with an annual lump sum. It's of no use trying to borrow more from the bank, as I have given them very particular instructions. Nor can you get additional funds from Belinda, for she must go through a maze of signatories to get any money at all, the amount set aside for her necessities being sent to her creditors direct.

As for Lustings, the bank has agreed to buy it, and hold the money in trust for Edward and Edwardina. Belinda shall then have the house to live in for as long as she likes, and when she dies, or if she should choose to live in some other residence, the property shall revert to the bank. As for Neddy and Eddie, they will come into the rest of their legacies when they turn twenty-one. If you are still alive then, which is doubtful, given your current mode of existence, I have instructed the officers at the bank to employ whatever means they deem necessary to see that your children's money does not find its way into your pocket.

This is all for the best, Charles, as you are well aware, and in case we shall not meet again on this earth, I here wish you a fond adieu.

Your loving sister,
Arabella

After placing this letter in the post bag, she drifted slowly through the house, visiting each of its rooms. The situation in which Arabella currently found herself was distressing for several reasons, but principal amongst these was the thought of losing her home. She had sworn allegiance to Lustings, to its lofty ceilings and polished floors—had dedicated the domestic energy and maternal devotion to it that would otherwise have gone into making a family. Arabella had been very happy here and had never had any doubts about her choice of residence, though her friends had been dubious at first.

"Lustings!" they'd cried in alarm. "But, my dear! The place must be over a hundred years old! Surely old Glen*deen* can afford to get you something more up-to-date! Wouldn't you prefer to live in a town house? Ever so smart, and so much more convenient to everything?"

"No," said Arabella. "I wouldn't."

She had first seen this house as a child of nine—a formal miniature manor of four floors, symmetrical to a fault—and the youthful Arabella had thought, as she gazed upon it with the first stirrings of obsessive passion, that it looked like a child-sized house for full-sized people.

It had been foundering in a state bordering on dereliction when the duke had first given it to her, and she had painstakingly, over time, "brought out its bones." Even the house's most vociferous detractors had reluctantly to admit that Lustings was now a most charming, most comfortable, most delightful house in every way.

And now Arabella was going to lose it. Not from her own folly, which she could have accepted, but owing to a set of circumstances with which she herself had had nothing to do. She reflected on this whilst ascending the stairs to her room. It simply wasn't fair, and in her heart, despite all she could do to prevent it, Miss Beaumont felt the seeds of bitterness crack open and begin to sprout.

This staircase had once been in bad repair, but she and her

architect had designed a new one—a graceful spiral—and the stairwell now glowed with the hues of pale roses and soft clouds. A spiritually sensitive houseguest had once observed that traversing the risers, when the sun shone down through the round skylight and past the pendant lantern, was like exploring the inside of a nautilus shell or traveling back through time, to the beginnings of life itself.

Her bedroom welcomed her, too, with that same tranquil beauty that had greeted her when she'd opened her eyes that morning. In the short time that had elapsed since then, however, everything else had changed. The freest woman in London now faced the close confinement of a prison cell. Where she had recently felt intensely, joyously alive, now she faced almost certain death, and in a matter of *weeks*. The contrast between two hours ago and this moment was almost more than Arabella could bear, and yet her bedroom, the outward manifestation of her inner world, had only grown a little brighter with the sun's transit. Its cool and complementary shades of blue—French blue, periwinkle, lavender—soothed her, though only slightly, by virtue of their contrast with the warm, apricot walls.

"Why don't you put up a nice paper?"

Her sister had asked her that once.

"If there were such a thing, I would," Arabella had replied.

Now she pictured what they had both been wearing that day; how Belinda had worn her hair. Memories, even little ones, had suddenly become terribly important.

Above the dresser containing her nightgowns and nightcaps and . . . things (the tools of her trade) hung a painted wooden fruit bat, a gift from her uncle Selwyn. It was beautifully carved, with removable wings, and Arabella had placed it beneath a gold-framed Japanese block print of evening foliage and insects, against an enormous, peach-colored moon, as if the bat had just flown out of the picture or were about to be absorbed into it.

The room's focal point, though, was the bed, surmounted by a crown of gilt wood, with acanthus leaf details and pendant pearl teardrops. Cascading from this was a quantity of blue-violet silk, divided into two sections and held open at the sides with spears of gilt wood. The lining, thus exposed, was spangled over with gold foil pineapples. In the open space between the draperies hung a round portrait, in a gilt frame, of a pretty young woman—no one in particular, although Arabella called her Venus—given her by the artist, Thomas Lawrence. He said that he wanted her to have something from him that could look at her whilst she was naked. The bed itself was a downy, private nest of plump pillows and smooth summer coverings. One could scarcely conceive of a more comfortable place of work.

She lay down upon it now and gazed at her white marble fireplace, at the two gold wood and blue velvet chairs that faced it, and through the open windows to the garden, with its shady trees and glorious roses. Tears sprang to her eyes as she listened to the lilting strain of birdsong—her world was so beautiful. And she had so little time left in which to enjoy it.

I wonder what it's like to hang? Arabella wondered, sadly stroking the pineapple fabric. Will it be like choking on a piece of steak, or does it actually hurt?

She rose and passed into the adjoining dressing room. This space had no windows but was sumptuously carpeted and nearly as large as her bedroom. Here she stored the magical hats and gowns and the bewitching accessories that so beguiled her clients. Every single thing in this room, each fan, each brooch, had a beloved memory attached to it. I'm growing maudlin, she thought, and yet, in the circumstances, there was nothing else she could be.

Arabella finished her tour of the house and drifted outdoors. Her heart-shaped property was bordered by two leafy avenues, which joined a circus at the apex where the entrance gate was. And what a gate! Two towering masterpieces of the ironmonger's art, anchored in an imposing structure of red brick and frothy plaster flourishes. It always gave her a shiver of pleasure to drive through this portal, for it made her feel like a princess. Every time.

On my final trip across this threshold, she resolved, I shall shut my eyes and not open them again until I reach the prison. She then made her way round the back to the kitchen garden, where her tour ended, and where she was eventually discovered by her sister, weeping amongst the pumpkins.

"Here you are, dearest!" cried Belinda, slightly out of breath, for she had run all through the house in search of her. "Oh, look at you, poor darling! You could almost be Cinderella, except, of course, your everyday frock is much nicer than hers was. Look what I have!" And she waved a piece of paper, like a child with a small flag.

"It couldn't possibly interest me, whatever it is," said Arabella, blowing her nose and tucking her handkerchief back into her bosom. "You must be very brave, Bunny. Something dreadful has happened."

"Yes, I *know*; the princess has told me all about it."

"How does she know?"

"Her servants told her."

"But how did *they* know?"

"Oh, they had it from the prince regent's servants, I expect."

"I see," said Arabella. "I must remember to remember about the omniscience of servants."

"But look, Bell!" cried Belinda impatiently. "This will *help!*" She threw herself down beside her sister, quite heedless of the soil and the earwigs, and showed her the document. "You see? It's a copy of a letter from Lord Sidmouth!"

Belinda was adorable. Shorter than her sibling and plump in all the right places, she had dark hair and dimples, and enormous violet eyes. Outwardly, the two young ladies scarcely looked like sisters. Yet they were twin spirits, for all that.

"What does it say?" asked Arabella listlessly.

"It orders the magistrate to assist you with your investigation!"

"What investigation?"

"The investigation which you will conduct, in order to discover the *real* murderer!"

"Oh, don't bother me with this now, Bunny. I have neither the time nor the inclination for silliness. I shall die soon. Can you understand that, dear? I am about to be executed, whilst you play about in a fairy-tale world!"

"And if I do," Belinda retorted, "who was the one read me all those fairy tales when I was small?"

"You're *still* small," said Arabella, smiling.

"When I was a child, I mean: My sister did! You should know better than anyone how this is to be borne!"

"Go gallantly to the gallows, do you mean? And then come back as a ghost and whisper the real murderer's name through the wind in the grass?"

"Oh. I don't know that one. No, I was thinking more along the lines of 'Clever Hans' and 'The Brave Little Tailor,' " said Belinda. "You're a strong, practical person, Bell, except when it comes to looking after yourself. Now, I don't often put my foot down, but I absolutely refuse to allow you to lie out here, wallowing in the vegetable marrows, when you should be girding on your sword and preparing for battle! Here! Read this!"

She thrust the letter at Arabella:

To: The Hon. Jotham Sanderton, Magistrate, and To Any Others Whom It May Concern:

Know ye by the order of His Lordship, Henry Addington, First Viscount Sidmouth and Home Secretary of the Realm, that the bearer of this letter shall be allowed to conduct an investigation into the murder of Euphemia Ramsey, deceased, and is entitled to the full cooperation of the law, including its support in the matter of uncooperative witnesses.

This letter to remain in effect until the 30th day of June, 1811.

And Sidmouth had signed it, with even more arrogant flourishes.

"Well, it does appear to have merit, at that," mused Arabella. "If I may go wherever I want, and question whomever I want, perhaps I *can* find a way out of this. . . . You know, Bunny, dear? I think you may have hit upon a terrific idea!"

"Do you? Oh, good, because I think so, too! You're a lot more clever than most of the people who run things, and *somebody* with a brain certainly needs to find out the truth! Who better than yourself?"

Arabella glanced at the letter again. "But Sidmouth?" she asked. "You actually saw the home secretary? I find that man completely and utterly disgusting!"

"So did I," said Belinda quietly. "And try as I might, I can't get the taste out of my mouth!"

Comprehension dawned in Arabella's gray-green eyes. "Oh, darling!" she cried, embracing her sibling with tender affection. "I am deeply touched! You have gone to great lengths on my behalf!"

Her sister reflected. "No, not really. No more than four and a half inches, I should say. The length wasn't the problem, you know; it was the—"

"I *do* know, dear. Believe me. Well, come along, silly Bunny—you can rinse your mouth out with port."

In the dining room, Belinda helped herself from a sideboard decanter, and then, because they were alone, she threw back her head and gargled unbecomingly.

"Shocking waste of good port!" she muttered, after spitting into a finger bowl and wiping her mouth with the back of her hand.

"I don't begrudge it in the least, I assure you!" said Arabella. She took the omnipresent pencil stub from behind her ear and began scribbling notes on the back of Sidmouth's letter.

"What are you doing?"

"Drawing up a list of persons with whom I should like to speak."

She replaced the pencil, folded the letter into quarters, and thrust it into her bosom.

"Where do we start?" asked Belinda.

"Domestics."

"Come again?"

"Domestic servants," Arabella explained, ringing the bell. "We have already seen how swiftly they acquire and relay information, and I've a notion that my own staff may prove invaluable in this matter. Oh, there you are, Mrs. Janks, dear. Would you assemble the staff in the drawing room, please? I wish to make an announcement."

The housekeeper's summons threw the staff into a mild panic.

"What's this all about, then?" whispered Doyle. "Are we to be dismissed? Is she closing up the house?"

"I dunno," muttered Fielding, "but there was p'licemen

'ere this morning, wantin' to take 'er away. The duke wouldn't let them, but maybe . . . D'ye think she's . . . ?"

"Shh! Here they come!"

The Misses Beaumont entered the room, with their arms twined round each other's waists, and faced the line of servants. Nobody curtsied, though; Arabella despised that sort of thing and wouldn't allow it.

"Well, you may as well know, if you don't already, that I stand accused of murdering Euphemia Ramsey on the night before last, or thereabouts."

The staff broke into indignant expostulations.

"But you was *here*, ma'am! And the duke was here with you!" Doyle cried. "Why, everyone knows you has breakfast in bed after you been workin', and hasn't it been myself bringin' it in t' you these past three days?"

There was general assent at this, and emphatic nodding of heads.

"Quite," said Arabella. "But for reasons which I cannot go into, that fact is not to be made public."

"Are you geeving us notice, madam?" asked the cook.

"No, I'm not, Mrs. Moly. Not yet, at any rate! I've called you all together to ask for your help; I have been given leave to conduct the murder investigation myself. I only have till the end of the month, though, and as much as I'd like to, I can't be everywhere at once. So I'm counting on all of you to be my extra eyes and ears. Miss Ramsey was killed with that paper knife that went missing from the library a week ago. Try to discover, if you can, who took it. I give all of you leave to quit the house whenever you wish to follow up on any ideas you may have on this matter, and if you find anything out, please report it to me at once, whether I'm dining, or having a conversation, or sleeping or anything. I shall need to know immediately."

"What if you're . . . working, ma'am?" asked the house-keeper.

"Oh! Good point! In that case, you must knock thrice, and rattle the knob. Are there any further questions?"

"Does this mean we won't be going to Bath, miss?" asked the cook's helper.

"Yes, Crouch. I'm afraid that it does."

Chapter 4

A TEMPLE IN THE TROPICS

*In which Arabella shares dessert with a Horny
Pheasant and insults His Royal Highness.*

The sisters were taking their ease in the aviatory temple—
Arabella tuning her lute, Belinda sewing—when Mrs.
Janks arrived unexpectedly with a newspaper draped over her
head, and a tray, a carefully covered tray, of strawberries and
cream.

"'Nobs and genteels . . . Do not sup between meals,'"
quoted Arabella piously, setting her instrument down.

The housekeeper's face was expressionless.

"Is that right, miss? I shall just take this away then."

But as she bent to retrieve the tray, Arabella grabbed on to
one end of it.

"*Don't* . . . touch that, Mrs. Janks!" she said, her tone low,
her expression threatening. "Not if you value your life!"

"You'll get fat, Bell," chided Belinda, who wasn't permit-
ting herself to have any. "And then we'll have to start calling
you 'Ara-belly.'"

Her sister appropriated the tray, snarling at Mrs. Janks
like a hungry jaguar. The housekeeper gave a triumphant, "I-
thought-as-much" kind of noise and left them, winding her
way through the giant bromeliads and clutching the newspaper tightly over her head.

"Why is that a bad thing?" asked Arabella, lining a bowl

with sugar biscuits and spooning strawberries into the middle of it. "I don't know what your lovers are telling *you,* Belinda, but *mine* always encourage me to put on flesh. They like to know whether they're sleeping with a man or a woman, you see, and a bony woman might easily be a boy; it's hard to tell, in the dark. Besides," she added, liberally sprinkling her bowl with sugar and drenching the contents with cream, "strawberries are good for you, and when you've got what I've got, it doesn't matter if you're fat or old."

"No? Not even old?"

"Well, old, perhaps," said Arabella, as she thought of Euphemia, "but not fat. Anyway, I should think you would be happy to see me eat like this. Most women, faced with the gallows, would not be able to choke down more than a few spoonfuls of broth."

"Does this mean that you're confident of a positive outcome?"

"Possibly. On the other hand, it might mean that I'm storing up memories—"

"—and fat."

"Yes, and fat, to sustain me during my coming incarceration, where I expect to be manacled so closely to the wall that I shan't be able to reach the stale bread and tainted water placed for me on top of a large rock."

"Oh, don't, Bell! I can't bear it! You know that your friends and I will all come to visit you often, laden with food baskets—*Wait!* Don't eat my strawberries, I've decided I want them, after all."

"Fine," said Arabella. "I'll ring for more, then."

The aviatory at Lustings may have been the only room of its kind in existence. For Arabella, wanting both a large aviary and a sizable conservatory, yet not wishing to alter the symmetry of Lustings's architectural lines, had combined two purposes in one. She had had to borrow space from the drawing room to achieve it, but the final result seemed well worth the sacrifice; Arabella's aviatory was a tropical Eden, a lush wilderness of rubber plants, banana trees, orchids, and lianas, populated with a profusion of jewel-bright birds. The remarkable room was accessed from the passage via a tiny antechamber, with a tile floor of pseudo-Pompeian design and a stand full of gray umbrellas. The hazards of walking beneath avian fauna being clearly understood, these useful articles served to protect visitors from droppings after they passed through the revolving door into the aviatory direct. But once the center of the room was gained, these were no longer needed. For Arabella had thoughtfully installed a little round temple there, with four pillars and a domed roof of opaque blue glass, where guests might read or play cards without fearing for their apparel. Indeed, on one famous occasion, a game of whist took place here, with the players devoid of garments whatsoever. But clothing aside, which is where it was placed on that occasion, it cannot be a pleasant task to remove digestive residue from one's hair.

Before we return to the Beaumonts, I beg that the reader will allow me to say a word on the subject of the aviatory's fauna. Here one might encounter species found nowhere else in the British Isles, all the birds having been either sent or brought to Arabella in person from her world-traveling admirers, and all thriving happily in the enormous glass room with the sixteen-foot ceiling. I shall simply list a few of them, for their names are as evocative as any close description that I could devise: emerald toucanets, coppersmiths, and fire finches; violet ears, paradise whydahs, nutmeg mannikins, and Peking nightingales; diamond doves, hoopoes, blue-chinned flowerpeckers, golden-fronted fruit suckers, and cocks of the rock.

There were no parrots, though, for parrots squawk so loudly and incessantly that one cannot have a conversation, and conversation was the one thing without which Arabella could not do.

"You seem to be spending more and more of your time with the princess, nowadays," she said, biting into a biscuit and talking with her mouth full. "I miss you dreadfully when you're away, Bunny. The house seems so empty."

"I miss you, too," Belinda admitted, spooning up the last of the cream in her bowl, "but the princess is so demanding. She has me going out to see her nearly every day, and Montagu House feels so queer now."

"I imagine it is much changed?" asked Arabella.

"Yes and no. They have cleared out all the specimens and antiquities, and replaced them with hideous furnishings, but the rooms themselves still have a museum-like feel about them. And of course, entry is still free to 'Curious Persons.' *Very* curious persons, some of them are. It is odd, though, to sit in the dining room and remember when it used to be the hall of mammals. Or to recall those rainy afternoons when Nurse used to take us to see Egyptian mummies in the room that is now Caroline's library. I don't even know why she bothers to have one."

"An Egyptian mummy?"

"A library. The woman *never* reads, and her ignorance is apparent every time she opens her mouth."

"Well, perhaps she isn't comfortable reading in English. I know I shouldn't like living in Brunswick and being forced to read German."

"Don't be contrary, Bell! Caroline could have German books, if she wanted them."

"What sort of books *does* she have, then?"

"What would you guess?"

Arabella smiled as her eyes roamed the ceiling. "Oh, multiple-volume sets of the history of dentistry, bound in calf with gilt edges. Something which looks very grand upon the shelf, that nobody in his right mind would ever think of cracking."

"You have got it, exactly! Actually, it's a history of engi-neering, but the concept is correct. It's a shame; all those lovely walnut bookcases, being put to such a pointless use. She might at least keep her naughty picture books in them. She is quite partial to those."

The young ladies having stuffed themselves, Belinda opened her workbasket once again, extracted a chemise from the in-terior, and applied herself to her latest project. The sly little puss had recently created a curious device: thin, Capiz shell disks, one inch in diameter, pierced along the rims at regular intervals to admit the insertion of a needle and thread. On the top of each disk, a length of satin piping described a cir-cle, with a glass bead fixed inside it. When two of these were sewn to the front of a chemise and worn beneath a gown, the effect was highly provocative.

Belinda had used an experimental pair to good effect the last time she attended the opera and was now embarked on a program to attach them to all of her undergarments. She had proposed to do the same for her sister, but the offer was gra-ciously declined, for Arabella was averse to advertising and regarded all such blatant displays as vulgar.

"Do you think *me* vulgar, then?" Belinda had asked.

"I do not judge others."

"Yes, you do! You do it all the time!"

"Yes, I suppose I do."

"And *do* you think me vulgar?"

"No. I think you . . . young. And absolutely delightful!"

This was true, Arabella told herself. She did *not* think Be-linda vulgar; she merely thought that her invention was.

"Have you any ideas?" Belinda asked presently.

"About what?"

"Well, on how to go about this investigation, on what to do first."

"I have already taken care of that."

"You have?"

"Yes. First I gave way to despair—or, no, first I put my affairs in order and wrote to Charles. Then I said good-bye to the house and the garden, and *then* I gave way to despair. So all that is out of the way. And as you know, I have advised the servants to keep their ears open."

"Be serious, Bell. What will you do next?"

"Go to bed, I suppose. Without the duke. I wonder whether I shall miss him?"

"*Bell.*"

". . . And then tomorrow, I thought we might take in the auction."

"Auction?"

"Of Euphemia's effects. The one her creditors are staging in Soho Square."

Belinda was mystified. "How do you know that?"

"I saw it in *The Ragpicker*. Will you come with me?"

"Of course, but what good will it do?"

"It mightn't do any. On the other hand, we may discover a clew, or meet the murderer, or . . . who knows? I might even get my elephant back."

Arabella was, by and large, a practical person, but she was an avid art collector and occasionally became attached to certain pieces out of all proportion to their monetary value. One of these objects had been an elephant, fetchingly fashioned of heavy, dark-red glass, which she'd seen in a shop window and had teazed out of one of her earlier lovers—she no longer remembered which one—while they were strolling down Bond Street. Her brother, Charles, had subsequently lost the elephant in a game of piquet—to Euphemia Ramsey. When Arabella had offered to buy it back, Miss Ramsey refused to part with it. This, in fact, had been the unofficial cause of their original falling-out.

A Horny Pheasant had entered the temple with stately tread and now stood looking up at Arabella with an expectant expression. Tragopans were alpine, rather than tropical, and they did not, in their natural habitat, eat things like sugar biscuits. But this one had adapted wonderfully to life in the aviatory, ingesting whatever was on offer there.

Arabella smiled at him. "Hello, Randy," she said affectionately. "Inflate your horns." Two azure, horn-like feathers on the sides of his head sprang to prominence, and the terra-cotta-colored bird raised himself up to full height, showing off the rest of his brilliant blue mating equipment. He should have done this even if Arabella had *not* asked him to, but it delighted her to pretend that the bird was responding to her wishes, and she rewarded him with half a biscuit.

"Euphemia knew how much I doted upon that elephant," said Arabella, "and of course, it meant nothing to *her*. She kept it just to vex me. But why should she want to do that? We were friends . . . in a way."

"Maybe she was getting even with you for your having stolen the duke."

"Nonsense. Women in our profession always share clients."

"Perhaps this was different. Perhaps Euphemia felt the same way about the duke that you felt about your elephant."

Belinda carefully kept her eyes on her sewing, for one never knew how her sister was liable to react to personal criticism. Sometimes she was perfectly reasonable about it. Other times . . . not so much.

"Well, if she did," said Arabella, "it has served her right: Courtesans cannot afford to become attached to men. Anyway, I won in the end, didn't I? I got the duke."

"You haven't got him now," said Belinda quietly. "He's going to be married to Julia van Diggle in October."

Arabella was thunderstruck. "What! To van Diggle? I hadn't heard that!"

"It was in *The Morning Post*. So you have neither the duke, nor the elephant, it would seem."

Belinda was too kind to add, "And it looks as though Euphemia might be the winner," but she thought it just the same.

"Come," said Arabella, rising from the table and opening her umbrella. "It is time for our constitutional."

Every day while the good weather held, the sisters were wont to walk or ride in the park for the good of their health. That was one reason, of course. The other was to show off to an admiring public. For successful courtesans want to keep themselves foremost in the hearts, the minds, and the wallets of all clients, actual and potential.

From the age of sixteen, Arabella had made her own way in the world as a highly paid woman of pleasure. She was not ashamed of it, for she loved her work and given different circumstances would doubtless have pursued the same course without charge to her partners. Hers had been a rich existence, full of glamour, excitement, and moments of pure happiness. Because Arabella wasn't just a courtesan—she was *the* courtesan. When she went out, crowds parted to let her pass. On the nights she attended the theater or the opera, the quizzing glasses were all turned toward her box, rather than the stage. Newspapers reported on her activities, reprinted the menus for her parties, described the way she decorated her house. The fact that she could not be presented at court, or attend social functions where respectable ladies were gathered, or be friends with virtuous women bothered her not a whit—for the men of the *ton* knew no such social restrictions, and as far as *they* were concerned, Arabella was the most desirable creature on two legs . . . or off them, which was even better. England's most amusing, talented, and intellectually gifted men had been proud to call her friend, and she in turn had been delighted, amused, and spoiled by them. Taken all round, it had been a most satisfactory arrangement. But those days, it seemed, were drawing to a close.

Today, the sisters had decided to take their walk in Queen's Garden. They took the carriage from Brompton Park, but the weather was so fine that Arabella insisted upon getting out and walking the last bit. Perhaps it *was* the weather, but perhaps she also wished to see whether the public's attitude toward herself had altered since the murder. As the Beaumonts walked down Lower Grosvenor Place, people passed them by without a glance. Arabella was stung, but Belinda wasn't.

"It isn't us, Bell. Look—everyone's headed toward the Chelsea Road. Something must be happening there. Let us go and see."

Sure enough, as they turned onto the Chelsea Road they unexpectedly encountered a vast crowd lining the street on both sides. Heads craned, eyes strained . . . all attention was focused in the direction of the waterworks. And here was the odd thing; everyone was silent. The rumble of a carriage could be heard approaching, and the next moment eight magnificent white horses appeared, pulling the ornate golden coach of the prince regent himself.

The crowd stood mute, with their hands at their sides. Nobody cheered or waved a hat. As the coach neared the sisters, Arabella shouted, "Get stuffed, you fat git!"

"Who is that person?" snarled the prince regent.

"Arabella Beaumont, Your Majesty," Lord Worcester replied. But his words were nearly drowned out by a swelling crescendo of boos from the populace, for Arabella's insult had acted like a clarion call on a company of soldiers. More insults were hurled. So were eggs, and vegetables.

A turnip struck the carriage window just as Lord Worcester shut it.

"By heaven, Worcester! I miss the old days!" observed the regent.

"Old days, sir? Which ones, in particular?"

"When monarchs could chop off the heads of anyone they liked!"

"And what did they do to people they *didn't* like?"

"Oh, stop it, Worcester; you know what I mean."

"Your Highness is desirous of decapitation for persons who shout insults, or throw turnips, no doubt."

"No—that is only for anyone who displeases me in a *small* way. For those who dare to offer insulting remarks I should insist upon drawing and quartering, preceded by semi-evisceration and partial burning. Decapitation's much too good for 'em!"

Chapter 5

MADE FOR A CHINESE SULTAN

*In which Constance provides a clew . . . perhaps,
Mr. Kendrick obliges the ladies with lemonade,
Oliver Wedge introduces himself, and Arabella
is reunited with her elephant.*

E arly the following afternoon, Arabella was on the point of
entering her carriage when she recognized the two Bow
Street Runners of the previous morning, approaching with
their hats off.

"Beg pardon, miss," said the dark one. "I wonder if we
might have a word?"

"Certainly, Constable. What is it?"

He bowed. "The name's Frank Dysart, miss; and this is
Thomas Hacker. We've been officially assigned to your case."

Constable Hacker was trying not to leer, but he evidently
remembered Arabella's invitation to come and see her when
this matter was over and couldn't help thinking about that.
Thus it was the suspect herself who was obliged to set the
professional tone.

"I see," she said coldly. "And this concerns me, how?"

"We have been instructed to keep a watch on your house
when you're in it, miss, and follow you whenever you go out
of it."

Arabella was on the brink of losing her temper when Belinda put her head out of the carriage window.

"Show them your letter, Bell!"

"My what?"

"Your *letter*. The one from Lord Sidmouth. Perhaps these fellows may be of service to us."

At the end of ten minutes, it was established that the officers could watch Arabella's house and follow her about as much as they liked, but that she might also employ them in running case-related errands, as needed.

"I am about to leave for the auction now," said the suspect. "How do you propose to follow me? On foot?"

"Yes, miss. They don't call us Runners for nothing!"

"Of all the idiotic arrangements," she muttered as the coach passed down the drive. "How can I possibly concentrate with those two hanging about, waiting to drag me off to prison? It's ghoulish! I feel like Faust, with his devil escort ready to drag him to hell!"

Just now, Arabella was more annoyed than anything else, but her unflappable sister was more anything else than annoyed.

"That's one way of looking at it," said Belinda. "However, you will also be able to accomplish more, with four additional legs and, who knows, perhaps two additional minds, as well."

"I very much doubt that! Although I must admit I am rather out of my depth. I have absolutely no idea how one goes about solving a murder. The usual thing is to question witnesses, I believe. But in this case, it would appear that there weren't any."

"Keep calm, Bell," Belinda advised her. "You must allow events to unfold naturally."

"You're not worried at all, are you?"

"Well, yes, I am, as a matter of fact. We are getting off to a very late start. Suppose someone has already bought it?"

"Bought what?"

"You said you might find a clew at this auction, but we

have no idea what it could be, and now it might be gone before we get there."

"Yes, but if we don't know what it is, we shan't miss it, shall we?"

"Speaking of missing things," said Belinda, who had a fine instinct for avoiding confrontations, "will you miss the duke, do you think?"

"Not as long as I have Lustings."

"What . . . ? Oh! The house, of course! For a moment, I thought you meant—"

"I did. I meant it both ways. It's what's called a double entendre, dear." The act of one-upping her sibling seemed to put Arabella into a better mood. "I don't suppose I mind so very much about his engagement—though Julia van Diggle *is* an awful prig—but Puddles and I could scarcely be termed 'soul mates.'"

Indeed, they could not! The duke had been prepared to let her hang, rather than offend his stupid fiancée. Arabella was determined not to do so, of course, but she certainly could not be counting on his support. No, she would not miss the duke. In fact, she had already forgotten what he looked like.

"Besides," she added, "after six months of marriage to Julia, he'll be knocking at my door. I won't have the slightest idea who he is by that time, and he will have to court me all over again."

"It's just so inconvenient about the alibi," ventured Belinda.

"It certainly is! And Lady Ribbonhat has sent me a letter."

"That dreadful woman! What does she want?"

"What she always wants. Lustings. She's given me notice to quit."

"Has she grounds?"

"Not the slightest. But she seems to think she can make Puddles take the house back, once he has officially given me up."

"Oh, Bell! I think maybe she can! The duke is bound to be

swayed by his mother, now that he no longer has you as a welterweight!"

"What?"

"No, I mean a sash weight."

"Darling, you're not making sense."

"What do they call it, when there's a balance? And something, like a gold nugget or a handful of diamonds, rests on one side, and then you put a pound of butter on the other side?"

"A counter-weight?"

"That's it!"

"Well, yes. I am fairly certain that Lady Ribbonhat *would* prevail, if everything depended upon the duke's decision. Fortunately, that is not the case, though; Lustings is legally mine. No, the only reason I mentioned her is that I fear she will be poking her nose into everything we try to do, and thwarting us in any way she can. So we shall need to keep an eye out."

"Do you mean like this?" asked Belinda, sticking half her face out of the carriage window. (She could be deucedly silly sometimes.) "Oh! Look, Bell!" she called, still keeping one of her eyes "out." "It's Constance!"

Constance Worthington, London's most frivolous demi-rep, and perhaps Europe's, too, was jumping up and down and waving her handkerchief furiously at them from the kerb. Outlandishly attired as she was in a gauzy white gown of several filmy layers, which fell only as far as her upper calves, and crowned with a close-fitting bonnet, lavishly overdressed with lace, she was quite impossible to miss, and no one should have believed the Beaumonts had they claimed to have done so. Arabella reluctantly told her coachman to stop.

"What luck, my dears!" cried Constance as the footman handed her in. "Newton's has got in a new shipment of cash-

meres! I've only just found out about it so there was no time
to come round to you which is just as well because I shouldn't
have found you at home in any case although I'm sure Fielding would have told me where you'd gone but that would
have done me no good as I am on foot as you see, having once
again run out of ready. We must go to Newton's at once!"

"But, Constance," Arabella said when she was finally able
to get a word in. "Won't you miss the ball?"

"What ball?"

"Aren't you on your way to a fancy dress ball? You look
as though you were got up like a baby destined for the Chris-
tening font."

"*I* happen to think I look very sweet!"

"Hmm. I suppose you do, at that," said Belinda. "But your
accessories are all wrong, in any case."

"Are they?"

"Yes. There is no time to go back and change them now, of
course, but the next time you wear this sweet little *tout ensemble,* rather than carry a reticule and a fan, I should try a
stick of barley sugar and a rattle."

The Beaumont sisters watched with amusement whilst the
impertinence of this remark dawned upon Miss Worthington's
odd little mind and gradually began to reflect itself upon her
countenance.

"Belinda Beaumont," said she, once it had, shaking her
finger in the face of the young lady, "you would be well advised to keep a civil tongue in your head when addressing
your elders! Especially those who are born women!"

"One is not *born* a woman, Constance," said Arabella.
"One *becomes* one. And judging from your habits, speech,
and apparel, you haven't."

Before Constance had time to feel this, Arabella added: "I
shall be happy to drop you at Newton's, if you like, but Belinda and I have business elsewhere."

"Yes," said Belinda. "We are on our way to Euphemia's auction—it's today, you know, Constance, and we have to go, because Arabella might hang if we don't."

In a society where nicknames were the norm, no one ever referred to Miss Worthington as "Connie." It was too close to the improper sobriquet she'd been called as a child, which was, she said, responsible for her having taken up her current profession. A homely woman, with a prominent chin and ridiculous, little-girl chestnut curls, Constance generally dressed as if she were nine and always spoke in a voice of breathless excitement.

"Well, but they won't hang her *today*," she said. "Surely you'd rather go to Newton's, darling? Euphemia sold off all of her good things long ago! She couldn't have anything left that you'd want, unless—Oh! are you going to bid on your old paper knife, Arabella?"

"What?"

"Your paper knife! The one that sailor stole from your desk."

"*What?*" cried Arabella and Belinda together.

"What sailor are you talking about, Constance?" Arabella demanded. "Who was he, and why have you never told me this?"

"Well, I didn't *know* who he was, then, did I? When I saw him take your paper knife, I assumed he needed to open a letter or something!"

"Why would anyone suddenly need to open a letter in the middle of a party?" asked Belinda severely. "Did you think the postman, finding this sailor not at home, was directed to deliver his mail to him at Lustings? At night?"

"I don't know! I did not think about that. . . . It never occurred to me that he was actually going to *steal* the knife! Then later, of course, I assumed that he had, when I read that Euphemia was stabbed with it."

"For heaven's sake, Constance! What did he look like?"

"Who?"

"The *sailor!*"

"I don't know!"

"Was he tall? Short?"

"He might have been. I just didn't notice!"

"Can you recall anything about him at all?"

"I think . . . he had a pigtail."

"*Constance!! All* sailors have pigtails!"

"Don't be cross with me, Bell! That's extremely unjust of you! After all, I have not done so badly. I remembered that he was a *sailor,* didn't I?"

"We don't even know *that,*" groaned Arabella after they'd dropped their friend at the shops. "Constance might just as easily have imagined the whole thing, or dreamt something similar five years ago."

Belinda was torn between loyalty to her sister and her love of fine fabrics. She sat wrestling quietly with her disappointment and was barely listening.

"All we know for certain is that on the night of my party for Bob Southey somebody stole my paper knife, and three days later Euphemia was stabbed with it."

"Mmm-hmm," said Belinda.

"It is probably someone who knew and hated both of us. But not necessarily. There were lots of people at the house that night: friends, and friends of friends' friends. The thief might have been a complete stranger to me, who knew, nevertheless, of the enmity existing between his intended victim and myself. Lord knows *that* was no secret. But the whole thing might just as easily be an unfortunate series of coincidences."

"Hmm?"

"Well, it *could* be. For instance, supposing somebody steals my knife intending to sell it. The handle is sterling, after all. On his (or her) way to the dolly shop to hock it, this person stops to see Euphemia. They quarrel; Euphemia dies. And that is only one of any number of possible scenarios. Oh, Bunny, I begin to despair."

Belinda shook herself from her reverie.

"You mustn't give up, Bell," she said with quiet emphasis. "Take this one piece at a time, like that skillful dressmaker at Newton's. Keep it plain, yet artful. After all, when it comes to human nature, the simplest explanation is usually the right one."

"You want to go to Newton's, don't you?"

"Not if you need me."

"I need you."

"Then I shan't go to Newton's."

"But I shouldn't like you to feel deprived."

Belinda sighed. "When one must choose between being noble and gratifying one's immediate desires, it is sometimes difficult to know what to do."

"Yes," agreed Arabella. "When I find myself in such a position, I generally imagine my life as a book. And then I decide whether I would rather have it written: '. . . and so I went to Newton's and bought everything that I wanted there' or '. . . I accompanied my unfortunate sister on her errand, and provided her with such comfort as it was in my power to bestow.' "

"Mmm," said Belinda distractedly. "I wonder if Newton's has got in more of that lavender-colored cashmere, with the chevron pattern?"

The auction was being held in Soho Square, by permission, owing to both the fine weather and the close, unsavory atmosphere of the late Miss Ramsey's former residence. As Constance had said, Euphemia hadn't had much that was salable, but the auction was well attended just the same, owing to the extreme sensationalism of the murder. To the human species, the possession of something, however insignificant, that has once belonged to the victim of a famous homicide, or even a not-so-famous one, has great appeal. Once, long ago, a disgruntled gentleman attempted to blow up the house of his neighbor and blew himself up instead. The populace scrambled to collect the pieces of him that had rained down upon the neighborhood, and fought bitterly over the recognizable scraps, such as ears and fingers. This was not a famous event. In fact, most of my readers won't have heard of it. Yet the remains of the would-be arsonist were as valuable to his collectors as are the fragments of a saint to the priests who guard them. The secular morsels were widely supposed to work miracles, too, just like the blessed bits, and I am certain that they were every bit as effective.

Euphemia's auction had turned out the sort of crowd that would gladly have bid upon the poor woman's pickled ears had they been on offer, and here a reader might imagine the spectators to have belonged exclusively to a certain lowborn section of the population: unwashed, unschooled, and uncivilized. But that would be most inaccurate! People from *all* walks of life had come to Euphemia's auction. Frock coats and summer brocades mingled freely with simple broadcloth and verminous rags. Here one might see faces of that pure type of English beauty, the sort that puts one in mind of morning dew upon roses, but here, too, were toothless gums in wrinkled faces; fat, florid countenances; flap ears, sunken chests, and huge, hairy nostrils. Such a profusion of features! There were people who looked like princes, people who looked like pirates, walking corpses and balloons with legs—and that was just the women! In short, Euphemia's auction was like a masked ball held out of doors in the daytime. For there is greater diversity in the London populace than exists among all other types of creatures in the world!

It was a proper summer's day, very sunny and very warm. Nay, it was *hot,* and the ladies had all to put up their parasols. Some people were standing in the shadow of that great lump of ectoplasm that is supposed to be Charles II, a statue that looks as though it has been gnawed upon by mice and probably has been. Others sought relief in the scanty shade afforded by the stunted little trees. A few limber young men had clambered up the poles of the new streetlights and peered down at the girls from there with the aid of spyglasses, whilst mothers and nursemaids clung to children in an effort to keep them from wandering off. The square had been converted to a spontaneous kind of funfair, with food and drink stalls, jugglers, a fiddler, and an Irishman, who, using nothing but his own knee and a fistful of teaspoons, provided a lively percussive accompaniment to the bidding upon the stage. And weaving through the crowd like sharks through herring, the ever-present pickpockets and cutpurses were going about their usual business.

In London, this type of unplanned carnival is apt to spring up wherever there is a public event of any kind, and Arabella shuddered, remembering the same sort of scene at Jerry Abershawe's execution. She had been eleven, Charles fifteen, when their father had taken them to see the famous highwayman pay his dues to society, for Charles Beaumont Sr. was always keen to see a good hanging. He was also suspected of necrophilia, but that is neither here nor there.

"Let that be a lesson to you, Charlie," he had said afterward. "For if you cannot learn to stay out of trouble, you will end up just like Jerry there."

Mr. Beaumont had not included his daughter in his address, for who could imagine such a sensible young lady standing up on the gallows platform, facing the crowd with her hands bound behind her?

"Murder weapons! Genu-wine replicas of the knife what killed the courtesan!" cried a hawker with a tray suspended from his neck. The knives on offer even bore Arabella's initials. No one had yet recognized Arabella herself, who had wisely left her distinctive landau a few streets away and had walked over. Her protective bonnet and parasol provided further anonymity.

"It's just as well that Constance isn't here," murmured Belinda. "She would probably have bought one of those knives."

"Quite," answered Arabella. "With money she'd borrowed from *me*."

The crowds! The noise! The air of excitement! And all over the pitiful possessions of a poor dead woman, who had once owned jewels and carriages far beyond the means of her audience. But all these had gone years ago. Most of what remained was now corralled together in the "sold" area, having been purchased before Arabella's arrival: a bed with dusty hangings; two chairs with moth-eaten needlepoint seat covers; an old dining table, much scarred and stained; and some articles of apparel that had seen better days. One enterprising debtor had even cut the bloodstained bedclothes into six-inch squares and was charging a shilling apiece for them.

"Look 'ere, miss!" he said to Arabella, thrusting one such scrap, stiff with dried gore, under her very nose. "Slap that there a'tween two glass plates, frame it, 'ang it on the wall! Wot a conversation piece, hey?"

He had managed to sell all but two of them in a matter of minutes.

The remaining items had been laid out atop several de-hinged doors, which looked as though they had once been kicked in. Arabella walked up and down the rows, examining the sad little artifacts, but she failed to find any diaries or other writings that might have provided a clew to the killer's identity. At the far end of the last "table" were a few smaller lots, things like a powder box and hairpins, an ink pot and quills, and . . . a ruby glass elephant. Arabella's elephant. The sole survivor of Euphemia's ornament collection.

"Good efternoon, byoodivul leddies. May I be of service to your good selves?"

A foreign gentleman in richly striped robes, probably from the Levant, bowed low before the Beaumont sisters. He was carrying a paddle with the number 89 painted on it.

"Yes. Lot Thirty-Seven, if you please," said Arabella quietly. He bowed again and moved off into the crowd.

"I must have that elephant in my life," said Arabella firmly. "Did you see that man I was talking to, Bunny? He's a proxy bidder. When the elephant comes up, he'll raise his placard, and do the bidding for me."

"Why don't you just do it yourself?"

"Discretion, dearest. Imagine what will happen if the crowd finds out that Euphemia's supposed killer is here."

"He *is?*" cried Belinda in alarm. "Where?"

"Darling, *do* try to use that nice little brain that God gave you once in a while. I was referring to myself."

"Oh. I see. Look, Bell! It's Mr. Kendrick! Yoo-hoo! Mr. Kendrick!" Belinda waved her arm, inadvertently bidding two shillings five pence as she did so.

"Mind what you're about there," cautioned her sister. "Unless you really mean to buy Euphemia's curling tongs."

A pleasant-looking young man, in wire-rimmed spectacles and the garb of a country parson, began making his way through the crush toward them, his face lit up with a becoming smile.

"Miss Beaumont! Miss Belinda! What a pleasure! I have just come from Lustings. Your housekeeper said I might find you here."

He shook each of them by the hand in turn but maintained his hold of Arabella's fingers a trifle longer than necessary. And here the reader may wonder at the improbability of the Beaumont sisters knowing a man of the cloth. But the Reverend John Kendrick had gone to school with Charlie Beaumont and used to spend his school holidays with the family. On the very first of these visits, he had become smitten with Arabella, and in the intervening years had discovered, somewhat to his own surprise, that the youthful attraction had not only persisted but intensified.

"Good afternoon, Mr. Kendrick," said Arabella, smiling. "What news of our wayward brother?"

"I've neither seen nor heard of him for the past two weeks. Rumor has it he's gone to Southampton."

"Whatever for?" asked Belinda.

"Free food and lodging with the Bartletts, I'll be bound. But that is not the reason I was calling upon you." Here he lowered his voice, and Arabella instinctively adjusted her parasol, to create a more private and acoustically enhanced area in which to hear him. "I know something of your . . . present difficulties, and wish to . . . to put myself at your service. If there is anything I may do to help you, please name it. The sooner we absolve you of this despicable crime, the better I shall be pleased."

"As shall *I*," said Arabella. "It is too good of you, Mr. Kendrick. As a matter of fact, I hope to bid upon one of the lots here, and after that, I was thinking of calling at Euphemia's former lodgings."

Kendrick was scandalized. "The White House Brothel?" he asked, with an involuntary glance at the derelict building.

"Well, it's not a brothel anymore, you know. All the same, it looks rather forbidding, does it not? If you would be good enough to take us over there, my sister and I should be very glad of your company."

"By all means! You should not even have come *here,* you know, unescorted. If anyone should recognize you, there is no telling what might not happen! I really don't like the look of some of these foreign ruffians!"

Arabella laughed. "It's the English ones that worry *me*," she said. "But if by chance you're referring to the fellow in the red-striped robes, I have just engaged him to bid on an elephant."

She looked toward her proxy bidder and noticed a tall man near the pie stall who was regarding her with frank admiration. Another time, perhaps . . . but just now she was busy. Arabella turned away, that her parasol might deflect his gaze.

"An elephant?" asked Kendrick. "Whatever next? Shall this person undertake to be mahout, as well, and guide the beast, with you on its back, all the way to Brompton Park? I should say the fellow looks much fitter for the company of elephants than for the society of ladies."

"I consider every well-mannered man fit for my society, Mr. Kendrick. You shouldn't judge too much on outward appearances, you know."

She peeped over her shoulder and under her parasol. That man was still watching her. There was something exciting about him. Even at this distance.

". . . And as for mahouts," she continued, "I doubt I shall require one. *If* I get the elephant, which I mightn't, you know, I shall carry *it,* rather than the reverse. It can't weigh more than five pounds."

Kendrick continued as though he hadn't heard her: ". . . and I should be wary of that fellow over there, as well, the one in the pearl-gray hat, who keeps looking over at you. He is not—"

"Mr. Kendrick, I wonder if you would be good enough to get me a glass of lemonade?"

"Oh! And me, too!" cried Belinda eagerly.

Kendrick's expression resembled that of a man who has been made to *swallow* a lemon. Without peeling it. Naturally, he wished to oblige the ladies, but he was also loath to leave them unprotected in this throng. Of course, he was unaware of their official escort—the two constables, who stood drinking beer at a discreet distance.

"By all means," said Kendrick. "But I must ask that you remain on this spot, and not engage in conversation with any strangers." So saying, he left them.

"Now we shall have a breather," said Arabella to her sister. "My lot is coming up next, and it would have been just like Mr. Kendrick to stand here, quizzing the audience whilst I was trying to concentrate."

Up on the makeshift platform, the auctioneer took a last drink from the tankard at his elbow and banged his little ivory hammer, as a judge would, for silence. "Now, ladies and gents," he said. "Lot Thirty-Seven is a collection of stuffs taken from the bedside table of the late famous courtesan herself! I'm given to hunderstand that Miss Ramsey kept a collection of lost an' found hobjects in the drawer of this table, inhadvertently left on the premises by her customers. Hm! And curious things they are, too! Hold 'em up, Poole, has I calls 'em out: spectacles, a set hof upper false teeth, a gentleman's pocket handkerchief—hm! Looks hexpensive— with the initial G on it, a pocket watch, doesn't work, though, I've tried it, a naughty cameo ring, a miniature of a gentleman unknown, and . . . this is by far the gem of the collection, a large glass helephant. Made in China. Careful with that, Poole. Lift it up high so's they can all have a good look at it. It's exquisite, ladies and gents, is it not? Made for a Chinese sultan, that was. So what am I bid for this grand collection of things from the bedroom of the murder victim? Who'll give a pound?"

"A 'Chinese sultan'? Arabella murmured. "I didn't know there were any left!"

"Shh! Don't be horrid, Bell," whispered Belinda. "Not everyone's had your education!"

"No, indeed!" replied her sister. "I'll wager that the auctioneer doesn't know the first thing about pleasing wealthy perverts!"

Arabella's would-be mahout glanced over, and she held up ten fingers. He could now bid as high as ten pounds without the need of consulting her further.

"I'll open the bidding at one pound. Do I hear one pound?"

To Arabella's consternation, three other placards besides her own were raised by foreign gentlemen and waggled about.

"I hope you will pardon me, madam. But have I the honor of addressing Miss Arabella Beaumont?"

The voice was deep, cultivated, and seemingly rich with the promise of both intimacy and wild abandon. Arabella turned just as the pearl-gray topper was swept off and an elegant bow effected, so that her first impression was of the top of the hat owner's head: lustrous thick brown locks, with not a hint of baldness. Then he straightened, and she had a good look at his countenance for the first time. It was a *face*. A *real* one, with character, humor, and intelligence—not some bland mask that might serve just as well for a tailor's window mannequin as for a man.

"And, if you have, sir," said she, "what is your business?"

"Allow me to introduce myself. My name is Wedge. Here is my card."

Arabella read the pasteboard rectangle that he handed her:

O. Wedge, Esq.
Proprietor and Editor-in-Chief
The Tattle-Tale

"Hmm," she said. "What does the O stand for?"

"Oliver. As in, 'Have you seen all of her, Wedge?' But my . . . intimate associates call me 'O.' It gives me rather a thrill to lie abed nights, knowing that women all over London are crying out my name in their transports: 'Oh! Oh! *Oh!*' "

At this juncture, a well-bred, gently raised young woman might have called to one of those constables. But Arabella always appreciated wit. Naturally, she much preferred the spontaneous variety, but shopworn jests were nearly as good, provided that she had not heard them before. As for the constables, Hacker and Dysart were around, somewhere, but she didn't want them at all.

"The Tattle-Tale," said Arabella thoughtfully, and she quoted from an article in that morning's *Times:* " 'The filthiest, vilest pack of salacious lies ever to be printed in one go.' "

Wedge smiled. "Even so," he replied. "And please permit me to apologize for the fact that a woman of your charm and breeding, to say nothing of your delightful reputation for . . . generous hospitality, should be implicated in the loathsome business of murder."

"Three pounds," called the auctioneer. "Three pounds, anyone?"

Arabella's proxy held up his placard. She smiled at Mr. Wedge, very slightly. "This is my sister, Belinda."

Bunny, who had kept her distance, came reluctantly forward and proffered a hand.

"Charmed!" he said, shaking it cordially. " 'Rape of the Lock'?"

"I was named for the Pope heroine. Yes," she replied.

"And aptly, too! You seem just the sort of young woman who could slay a man with her eyes."

Belinda didn't like him. But her sister did. He stood about six-two and had the body and superb carriage of an athlete, though his face was not handsome in any conventional sense. His nose was large and rather quizzical—the sort of nose accustomed to pushing itself into private matters. His eyebrows were bushy, the eyes beneath them keen and intelligent. A weak chin produced the impression of a slight overbite, lending a touch of humorous affability to his otherwise powerful visage. In a time when gentlemen of fashion were spending considerable time and money having their manes curled just so, Wedge wore his thick brown hair straight, and a bit too long, perhaps. It suited him, suited him admirably, and he stood out from the herd in a way that was by no means disagreeable. His large, expressive mouth, with lips that seemed made for love, belied the intelligence of his eyes, the grace and power of his body. He exuded an animal vitality that made Arabella, experienced though she was, blush a little beneath her sunshade.

"Miss Beaumont," he said, "as a newspaperman, I am in a position to deliver you from your present difficulty, by swaying public opinion in your favor."

"And why should you want to do that, Mr. Wedge?"

"I could say it is because of your beautiful eyes—and they *are* beautiful—but you are too clever to believe that I would be motivated by that, alone."

"Well, then?"

"I have long been irritated by the halfhearted efforts of the London constabulary to dispense justice in this city," he said. "If I promote your cause and help prove your innocence, they will be made to look like the fools they are, and I can perhaps convince the authorities of our need of professional police protection. Tell me your story, Miss Beaumont, I beg of you, and I shall see to it that all of London rallies to your support."

Up on the stage, the bidding had now risen to seven pounds, and all but one of Arabella's rivals had dropped out of the running. Her proxy glanced at her again, and she held up four more fingers, her attention now divided between following the auction and listening to Oliver Wedge. But at that moment, the reappearance of John Kendrick, bearing down upon them with two lemonades, evidently struck the fear of God into Arabella's new champion, for he broke off mid-question and stared at the rector, dumbstruck.

"Wedge!" said Kendrick in a quiet but menacing undertone. "Begone, sir!"

At this same moment, the auctioneer's ivory hammer came down for the last time. "To number eighty-nine, eight pounds sixpence!"

Belinda gave a giddy little scream of joy. "Bell! Eighty-nine! That's you! You've got the elephant!"

"And thanks to you, Bunny," said Arabella between clenched teeth, "everybody here *knows* I've got it!" She lowered her head, that her bonnet might better hide her face, and when she looked up again Mr. Wedge had vanished without a word of good-bye, melting into the crowd like a pat of butter on a bowl of steaming porridge.

"Have a care, Miss Beaumont!" cautioned the rector. "That was Oliver Wedge, editor of *The Tattle-Tale,* and a thorough villain!"

"I know who he is, Mr. Kendrick," she said, accepting one of the lemonades. "I found him a perfectly affable, courteous gentleman, and quite sympathetic to my circumstances. Perhaps he will be kind enough to overlook your inexplicable rudeness in ordering him off, and use his considerable influence to help sway public opinion to my side."

Kendrick regarded her grimly. "I would not count on that if I were you. Wedge is a notorious blackguard who thinks of nothing but his own personal gain. He probably just wants to gather information for your obituary."

Chapter 6

"SHE GIVE IT T'ME AFORE SHE DIED."

In which Mr. Wedge and Constable Hacker reminisce;
Arabella makes a promise, receives a foretaste
of the future, and acquires a piece of Euphemia's
ephemera; and Mr. Kendrick denies himself,
that propriety might be satisfied.

"We got the knife, don't we? It's hers, innit? Well, I mean, it's an open-an'-shut case, is wut it is. They was enemies. Everybody knowed that."

Constable Hacker sat on the steps of the White House with his second pot of ale, while across the square Constable Dysart followed Arabella to her carriage . . . carrying her purchase for her.

"Not necessarily," said Oliver Wedge, repeatedly scraping his boot along the edge of the bottom step and checking the sole. "There might be a hundred other explanations. That's the problem with you Runners; you jump to conclusions before all the evidence is in, and nine times in ten you turn out to be wrong."

They were awaiting Arabella's arrival outside what had formerly been a prosperous brothel but was now little more than a run-down rabbit warren of decaying alcoves and passageways. Most of the windows were either broken or bricked in and much of the building was rotting away, but the landlady, Mrs. Ealing (who, she'd have you know, was *not* the former madam), still let a few of the unfurnished rooms. Up until last week, Euphemia Ramsey had been one of the tenants. She had first come to the White House over forty years ago, an innocent country girl in the company of a pimp, and had left a short time later, an experienced courtesan. Then, after a life of almost unimaginable glamour, she had returned, ruined by debts and alcohol, and now she was dead at fifty-three, murdered with a paper knife belonging to Arabella Beaumont.

Constable Hacker had put Mrs. Ealing on notice to open up the room again.

"Ever come here when this place was still doing business?" he asked Wedge.

The editor eyed him with disfavor. "It hasn't been operational for more than ten years," he said icily.

"I *know*. I ast if you was ever here *before* that."

Wedge stared up at the bricked-in windows, his expression equally blank. In his head, though, he was composing an editorial, blasting the lax morals and poor training of the London police. What an insolent dog this fellow was! Did he really suppose gentlemen to be in the habit of comparing amorous exploits with complete strangers? Strangers of the lower classes? Well, he'd soon see about that—Wedge had got the fellow's name and was planning to use it in the editorial.

"I only wondered," Hacker continued, "because I worked here as a boy, down in the dining rooms. You seem familiar."

Wedge reddened.

"Yeah," said Hacker. "I thought so. It wasn't the face, so much; it was the voice. You've got an unforgettable voice, you have."

"I think I remember you," said Wedge, peering at Hacker. "Weren't you the lad who used to bring steak and oysters to my room?"

"Aye: 'Roast beef rare and oysters raw!' " he mimicked Wedge's deep voice. " 'On the double, lad; on the *double!*' "

They laughed.

"Oh, but this was a grand place in the old days!" Wedge exclaimed, his hauteur washed away by shared memories and oyster brine. "Remember the grotto? And the coal hole?"

"I'll never forget those long as I live!" Hacker replied. "The things I used to see when they'd open the doors to take in a delivery!"

". . . and the skeleton room," Wedge said. "Where you would tell some unsuspecting girl you'd brought in from outside to pull the curtain, and when she did, the mechanical bone man would spring out and clasp her in his arms!"

"I liked that sofa," said Hacker. "The one where the straps flew out and buckled a woman in, soon as she sat on it. But I never understood the skelinton. I meanter say, what has skelintons got to do with rumpy-pumpy?"

"Sex and terror are close allies," said Wedge. "If you frighten ladies . . . or men, for the matter of that . . . so badly that they actually believe they're going to die, and then step in and save them at the last possible moment, their miraculous escape from death will make them feel that they must make a baby, at once."

He offered his snuffbox to Tom. "Some of the rooms were on the level, though," Wedge continued. "Lavish, even. I think I liked the bronze room best, but women usually preferred the gold. Well, they would, wouldn't they?"

The two men smiled, remembering.

"Bell—if you don't really need me just now," said Belinda as they walked back to the landau, "with Mr. Kendrick as your escort, and the two police officers . . . would you mind if I just went along to Newton's and tried to find Constance?"

Arabella sighed. "No, I suppose not. Have you got any money with you?"

"Some."

"Well, take a cab. Do not try to walk it. There are any number of rum-looking types on the streets today."

"Thank you, Bell!" Belinda cried, bestowing a hasty kiss on her cheek. "I'll be home for supper!"

"Wait, Miss Belinda," said Kendrick. "Let me get a cab for you. Constable, I am leaving Miss Beaumont, here, in your care."

Once the box had been safely stowed inside her carriage, Arabella lifted the lid and looked at her elephant. Why had Euphemia kept this back, even as she sold off all her other possessions? Because she liked it? Because it represented her triumph over Arabella? Or was it because it *reminded* her of Arabella, and of happier times the two friends had shared? Suddenly she felt a surge of tenderness toward her old foe.

"I shall find your killer, Euphemia," she whispered to the figurine. "I am doing this as much for your sake as my own . . . well, no, I'm not, but I *am* doing it for you, *too*."

With its indifferently tended square, deteriorating statue, and respectable homes standing cheek by jowl with brothels and doss-houses, Soho epitomized the little neighborhood that couldn't. Originally planned as an exclusive enclave for the upper classes, it had never quite realized those aspirations, and while undesirable tenants continued to pour in, conducting criminal activities and drastically decreasing property values, the few well-heeled inhabitants who lived there had begun to trickle out. The kindest thing would be to say that Soho had seen better days, but this wasn't strictly true. Even so, there were still a few celebrated citizens whose houses faced the square: Sir Joseph Banks, for example, president of the Royal Society and a great friend of Arabella's. It was Banks who had first got her started collecting exotic birds, and she thought how nice it would be to drop in on him now, for a cup of tea and a cozy discussion about beetles. But Sir

Joseph was undoubtedly gone to Bath or Tunbridge Wells for the summer—his house had an empty look. And even if he wasn't, courtesans did not pay calls, without invitation, at the homes of prominent gentlemen. Especially not married ones. Arabella turned, instead, toward the White House.

Imagine, reader, that you are standing in a nearly empty room, soiled with soot, unclean living, and the grime of ages, from which the last vestiges of Euphemia Ramsey's existence have been almost eradicated. A few petrified food relics and empty bottles still litter the floor; a rag remains stuffed through a hole in a broken window. If Miss Ramsey's spirit were permitted one last backward glance at her worldly domain before moving on to realms beyond this one, it would not have recognized any of these items as having been specifically connected with herself when she was alive. The pointless and the impersonal are all that remain of her fifty-odd years of existence. Soon these, too, will be swept up and disposed of.

Through the open door, a voice is heard, increasing in volume as its owner approaches:

". . . Removers left the place in a dreadful state, they did: Carted off all the poor thing's valyables for that there auction, and left all the trash behind! You come just in time, miss; my char's off takin' care of 'er ailin' mother today, but tomorrer I'm havin' her clean the place out so's I can let it to somebody else! Here we are, Constables, sir, miss. I doubt if you'll find anythin' in 'ere, but you're welcome to have a look."

The room stank of dry rot and mildew, which Arabella attempted to alleviate with snuff. She politely offered her box in turn to the two constables and Oliver Wedge but was thankful that the landlady, who remained shifting her weight nervously on the threshold, was sufficiently far away from the group to be tactfully excluded. Two pinches of snuff, caught up between those fat fingers, would have substantially de-pleted Arabella's supply, and the blend she preferred was an expensive one.

It was a grim little place. Several dark stains remained upon the floor and one of the walls. Small piles of rubbish lay strewn about, cobwebs filled the corners, and a host of small flies drifted erratically within the confines of two sunbeams, which served only to light up the dust. A hook protruded from the center of the ceiling: strange . . . or no, probably not. The place used to be a brothel, after all. A prop, or even a person, could have been suspended in a harness from a hook like that.

Poor Euphemia, thought Arabella. To have died in such a place as this! The dead woman had once been the most fa-mous courtesan of her time, even as Arabella was now. But when courtesans grew old and lost the freshness of youth, they tended to lose everything else, as well. There was a les-son to be learned, here. Of course, in this case, Euphemia's taste for gambling, drink, and ruinously expensive young men hadn't helped, but what else *could* she have done? Her glamorous life was over forever, and she had no family, no friends, no skills to fall back upon. Euphemia had been trapped. And even without being murdered, Arabella reflected, she could not have expected to live much longer.

She *was* murdered, though; she had suffered pain and ter-ror at the hands of someone who'd had no right to take her life, and Arabella was suddenly stung by guilt, a sensation to which she was unaccustomed. But she hadn't known Eu-phemia was living like this; how could she? When they had not even been on speaking terms? And what could she have done to help if she *had* known? Giving the woman money would only have hastened her down the path of self-destruction. It was a hopeless situation, no matter how one viewed it, and Arabella was determined—in the event that she survived the gallows—not to share Euphemia's fate.

From her post in the doorway, the landlady was giving her personal version of the tragedy for the hundredth time.

". . . and the constables, these selfsame young men as is standing here naow, ran over t' the bed, but it wasn't no use. She were as dead as come-ask-it, with the bed all soaked in 'er blood, and a great pool of the stuff on the floor. . . ."

"Thank you, Mrs. Ealing," said Arabella, handing her a shilling. "If I have any more questions, I shall come and find you."

After the landlady had gone, Arabella made a circuit of the room, gingerly prodding and lifting things with the tip of her parasol.

"Why have you come here, Mr. Wedge?" she asked of the man in the pearl-gray hat.

"Forgive the intrusion, but I overheard you say that you intended to visit this place, and I thought that I should see whether I might be of any assistance to you."

"I am looking for diaries, lists, letters, anything with writing on it," she said. "You may join in, if you wish. But I doubt very much whether you have actually come here to help."

"Why do you doubt me?"

"Because I know your newspaper. You just want a statement, do you not?"

"No."

"You don't?"

"I want a statement, yes; but I don't *just* want a statement."

"Well. I shall give you one. Not here, though," she said, glancing over at the Runners. Hacker and Dysart were standing against the wall with their hands behind them, staring off into space, and earnestly trying to give the impression of being somewhere else.

Wedge took her point readily. "Oh, quite!" he said. "Could you meet me at the Cabbage Moth, on—"

"Certainly not! The Cabbage Moth, indeed! I shall meet you at . . ." She took the pencil stub from behind her ear and wrote "Vauxhall" on the back of one of her calling cards, adding a date and a time, so that the constables should not know of her plan. Arabella almost never had occasion to use her calling cards for their intended purpose, but she found them invaluable for instances like this one.

"*That* is where I shall give you a statement," said she, handing him the card. "As for whatever else it is that you want, Mr. Wedge, we shall have to see."

"I am much obliged to you! But . . . couldn't you give me a brief statement now? Just a sentence or two?"

"Oh, very well. You may tell your readers that I am working hard to discover the murderer's identity, with the aid and full cooperation of the London constabulary . . . such as it is."

The constables made no sign of having heard her.

Wedge wrote this down. "And what are your current relations with the Duke of Glen*deen?* Is he assisting you, too?"

"I have nothing to say on that subject."

"Is it true that he has given you up in order to marry Julia van Diggle?"

"Really, Mr. Wedge! Where have you been? Their engagement was announced in *The Morning Post* today. I hardly think it *my* place to keep you informed of developments."

"I take it that you are no longer under the duke's protection, then."

He looked her straight in the eye. Arabella gazed straight back at him. And there is no way of knowing what might have happened next, for Mr. Kendrick entered the room at that moment and instantly assumed a belligerent stance, complete with clenched fists.

"Wedge! You villain! If I catch you sniffing around Miss Beaumont's skirts again, I shall call you out, sir! Leave this place at once!"

The editor turned on his heel, without acknowledging Arabella, and the vicar followed him up, to make sure that he left.

Here was a mystery! Why should Wedge so readily obey Kendrick's commands? Evidently, something had once passed between these two that accounted for this odd behavior. Arabella would have to inquire about it later.

"I was just leaving, Mr. Kendrick," she said upon his return. "There is nothing here of any interest to me. The removers were most thorough."

But as the group regathered in the passage, a door opened on the opposite side and a head in a torn cap was thrust out from it.

"Psssst! Missus! I 'eard you say you was investigatin' the murder."

"I am."

"Well, I can show you summat, but it'll cost ya."

"Come along, Miss Beaumont," urged Kendrick. "This person can have nothing to say to us."

"Not *you*," said the head. "It's only 'er I want."

"I wonder, Mr. Kendrick," said Arabella, "whether you would be good enough to question the landlady for me? I should like to know whom Euphemia was in the habit of entertaining here, and to get an account of her movements on the last night she was seen alive. Could you do that, whilst I speak to this individual?"

"I don't think . . ."

"Please, Mr. Kendrick?"

"I don't like to leave you alone in this place."

"I shan't be alone, with two of London's finest dogging my footsteps. Go and ask about it, do. I should be *ever* so grateful."

She smiled at him again, and Kendrick went, her obedient servant. Arabella turned once more toward the head.

"How much are you asking?"

"Twenty pounds!"

"Oh, bugger off!" growled Tom.

"No, no," said Arabella hastily as the head was withdrawn. "The officer did not mean that. I shall be happy to pay what you ask, provided you truly have something I can use."

"You can come in then. But mind, just you. I'm not havin' no coppers inside my room."

"It's all right, Mr. Dysart," said Arabella as Frank seemed about to force his way in. "One of you can stand here, just beside the door, and the other can wait outside the house, in case I try to 'escape.' I won't be a moment."

For the second time that day, Arabella was moved by the squalor in which she found herself. Euphemia's apartment had been cleared of all usable items, so the state of the room was perhaps semi-excusable. But this chamber was occupied by a living, breathing human being. Yet it resembled nothing so much as a compost pile, moved to the city and maintained indoors. Dear God. The stench in here was nearly overpowering! A wave of nausea swept over Arabella, and she thought for a moment that she was going to be sick. But the feeling passed when the woman handed her a book. Arabella immediately bore this to the window and examined it under the thin light that struggled through the grime-coated pane. It was some sort of ledger, clothbound, with most of its pages torn out. The few that remained appeared to be a record of various personal details pertaining to Euphemia's former clients: what they had liked, what they had paid her to do, and what she had thought of them.

"Where did you get this?" Arabella asked. And for the first time, she really looked at the woman. Skeletal, with loose, yellowish skin, the creature stood up in a filthy, sleeveless nightgown, scratching her arms. Corkscrews of brittle hair, which protruded from a ruffled mobcap, were pasted with sweat to her neck and forehead.

"She give it t'me afore she died. Said t' keep it away from the Runners."

The woman's breath stank. When she opened her mouth to speak, Arabella could see that she'd lost most of her teeth. Laudanum addict, Arabella thought. There could be no doubt. The pinpoint pupils of the eyes confirmed it.

"She did? Then why have you torn out most of the pages?"

" 'Twas like 'at when she give it t'me."

"You know where they are, though."

"No! I never seen 'un!"

"Well," said Arabella, handing back the book, "this is useless to me in its current condition. You find those missing pages, and then we can talk about price. Otherwise, I shall turn you in to the magistrate for obstructing this investigation."

As she turned to leave the room, the wretched woman gave an agonized cry.

"I don' *have* the pages, missus! I don't *know* where they be! I . . . I lied to you. She never give me this. I went in, didn't I? Went into her room as they was takin' the last of 'er stuff down to the square. This was lyin' there, on the floor, under a pile of rags and broken dishes. They didn' want it for the sale. Because it was tore. That's the God's truth, I swear it! But, if you could give me a few bob for this, just a few bob, missus. I've had nothin' to eat for three days!"

She wasn't crying, but the hopeless look in those eyes was infinitely sadder, like that of a half-throttled cat, waiting with resignation for the other half.

Arabella considered the ledger in the woman's hand. It was much stained and disgustingly smudged with food and wine and no telling what.

"All right," Arabella said, reaching into her reticule and pulling out a coin, "I'll give you half a crown for it."

Half a crown was a lot of money. Probably more money than this person had seen together in quite some time. Yet there was no reaction. She held out one apathetic claw for the coin, and Arabella pulled the ledger from the other one.

Dear God, she thought. Kill me when I'm young, if you must, on the gallows, even, but don't let me end like this!

"Are you all right, Miss Beaumont?"

She had come outside again, into the blessed sunshine.

"Of course I am, Mr. Kendrick. And you?"

"Yes, as you see—Did you get anything useful from . . . the neighbor?"

She showed him the violated ledger. Kendrick took it from her, opened the book to the first entry, and hurriedly shut it again.

"Where is the rest of it? Does she plan to charge you by the page?"

"No. She found it in this state. The removers left it behind, probably owing to its being damaged."

"Or," mused Kendrick, "the murderer might have nipped inside whilst the removers were busy, and torn out the pages pertaining to himself! Perhaps he pretended to *be* a remover."

Arabella stopped and looked at him. "You don't suppose that Euphemia was killed over something in this book?"

"Quite possibly. She may have known too much about someone who . . . someone of great political importance."

"I very much doubt it, Mr. Kendrick. This was a private business ledger, after all. No one would have known about the contents. Or, if they did, they would surely have destroyed the entire book, rather than remove some of the pages and leave the rest to be discovered later."

Kendrick shrugged. "There is no telling what some hypothetical person may or may not have done with the hypothetical missing pages," he said, smiling. "Anyway, the landlady was not much use, either. According to her, Miss Ramsey never had any visitors. Her clientele had abandoned her, you see; that was why she moved here in the first place."

"Well, but that is *something!*"

"Not really. The landlady has no way of knowing who comes in or goes out after dark, as her own apartments are in the rear of the building."

"Oh. Well, thank you for asking her, all the same. May I offer you a lift home, Mr. Kendrick?"

"That is very good of you, Miss Beaumont, but regrettably, I shall have to decline. It might be taken amiss if anyone should see you riding with me, unchaperoned."

Arabella smiled. "I appreciate your tact, but you and I both know that the lack of a chaperone is not what would shock people, unless, perhaps, it was *your* virtue they feared for. If any of your parishioners happened to see the rector of Effing riding in Arabella Beaumont's carriage, it might well cost you your career."

"Oh! But, I didn't mean . . . I . . ."

"That is all right, Mr. Kendrick, I am not offended," she said. "If my clients were threatening to take their business elsewhere because I sometimes kept company with a clergyman, you may be sure that you and I would be meeting with far less frequency."

Chapter 7

MUSTERD AND SOSAGES

*In which Arabella reads aloud, Belinda recovers from a
broken heart, the crime investigation notebook is
begun, and Arabella throws away her laudanum.*

From Easter to the middle of June, Arabella was accustomed to host intellectual gatherings at Lustings, where
she entertained some of the finest male minds in Britain,
twice weekly. No conversational topic was forbidden the
guests—provided it was interesting—and ideas that would
elsewhere have been condemned as heretical, treasonable, or
coldly scientific were frequently aired in the Lustings drawing and dining rooms. Thus Arabella's salons had been condemned from pulpits as far away as Aberdeen, whilst George
Canning claimed that at no other house in London could one
hear so vast a collection of remarkably good sense spoken at
one go.

"Bunny, dear," said Arabella. "Would you write to any
members of my salon who may still be in town? Explain the
situation—although I imagine everyone knows already what
it is—and say that, until further notice, we shall have to cancel the Tuesday and Saturday night dinners. I am going up to
my desk, and shan't be down to supper. Please ask Cook to
send up a tray at half past ten."

The boudoir at Lustings was a pleasant little dove-colored

nook off her bedroom, where Arabella did her best writing and thinking. In addition to the desk, there were two comfortable chairs, a small sofa, and a charming little French stove of pink porcelain. This was the place she had earmarked for her murder investigation headquarters: Here she was resolved to plot and ponder and map out strategies until the battle was resolved, in one way or another.

For her opening sortie, Arabella sat down and read the victim's ledger, right through. Euphemia was formerly very methodical when sober; each left-hand page featured a first and last name, the named person's address, and columns headed "Date," "Services rendered to," "Amounts paid," and "Client of."

"Client of"? These weren't just Euphemia's customers, then. (Odd!) On the right-hand page, the author had scribbled anecdotes about the client, along with personal remarks about his habits. Her grammar was poor, her spelling atrocious, and it was a pity that so many pages were missing, because the few that remained were quite interesting.

> *X liks to have his tows sucked while he attempts to send a stream of yurin up to the shandeleer. I won't have him over to the house again, as my servants have threatened to give notice rather than clean up his dredful meses and I can't say as I blame them neither. Still, X is a steddy customer and one of the few that pays reglar. So now I meet him at The Cabbage Moth, where I guess they doesn't mind about such things havin seen much worse.**

*The reader must pardon the substitution of capital letters for names in these entries, the publishers having no wish to be sued by any persons who may still be living.

Miss Ramsey had once commanded a magnificent household in Mayfair, staffed by an army of servants. That had been some years ago, of course, before she'd lost her looks and her money.

There was a paragraph on the previous Duke of Glen*deen*, Puddles' father, who had liked to do it standing up. The word "DISEASED" was written across the bottom.

Hmm, thought Arabella, I wonder whether he transmitted his disease to Lady Ribbonhat? That might explain a lot; perhaps her brain has gone all syphilitic.

Other entries had notations like "dull" or "obskyer" scrawled across the pages.

Y is so meen he makes his stockins do for another day by removing them and cleaning between his toes with his fingers. First he sniffs his stokings. Then he sniffs his fingers, and then he turns his stackings inside out and puts them back on agin. He can get through a week on just three pair, with a fourth for Sundays. When he wears boots though, he dispenses with stalkings altogether, saving even more on londry, but the man smells like a tanning factory.

Arabella noted with delight that Euphemia had mentioned stockings four times for this client, without ever once having spelled it the same way. One entry, which caught Arabella's attention particularly, pertained to Julia van Diggle. The duke's fiancée! Well, well. Miss van Diggle always passed herself off as a woman of irreproachable virtue, yet she had evidently participated in some highly imaginative group encounters with Euphemia and the French ambassador. This information might almost certainly find a practical use if Arabella were acquitted.

Eventually she came to an entry of several pages pertaining to herself. She had been half-expecting this, for Euphemia had been ever wont to hold a grudge. Still, the entry was slanderous in the extreme, and Arabella smiled to think that Euphemia was dead and couldn't show it to anybody.

That only strengthens the case against me, though, she thought, and the smile faded. Well. There was no sense in keeping *this* information lying about. She grasped the cover firmly with her left hand, tore out the three pages devoted to her own misdeeds with her right, and ripped them to bits. Then she wadded the bits into a ball and poked them into her pink porcelain stove.

There! Arabella straightened and stretched. Her body was *so* tired, yet her mind was as sharp as Euphemia's pen. She scanned the bookshelves above her desk, which held a phalanx of notebooks made expressly for her and used mostly for diaries. They were lovely things, with marbleized endpapers and gilt-edged pages of thick, creamy rag paper. She had had them bound in calfskin dyed all sorts of delicate colors: gray, lavender, pink, butter, sage green.

Arabella selected a pale-blue one for her notes and wrote "Crime Investigation" at the top of the first page. Then she checked her current diary on the date of her last party for a list of attendees. But this wasn't particularly helpful, as there had been simply heaps of guests and many had, as she'd said, brought large numbers of strangers with them. These people often arrived late and were never introduced to her. Arabella liked running a harum-scarum household for the most part. But this was one of the drawbacks.

There was only one name on her guest list that also appeared in Euphemia's ledger, that of Arabella's brother, Charles Beaumont.

Could Charles be the murderer? The possibility was almost too horrible to consider, and yet, if she were dead, he would come into a small annuity. Not much, but something. And he is always so desperate for money, she thought. But as desperate as *that?* Well, it did seem peculiar that he hadn't been round to see her, when he knew what straits she was in. In fact, Arabella had not seen or heard from Charles since her party, in fact.

Well, all right, it could be Charles.

She returned to her new crime investigation notebook. I'll have to shorten the name, she thought, and promptly came up with "CIN." The free associations for this acronym pleased her immensely, and she wrote up all the details she knew or could guess about the case so far:

Facts & Conclusions

1. *A person or persons unknown, or somebody in his/her/their employ, stole my knife during the party for Mr. Southey, and murdered Euphemia Ramsey with it less than a week later.*

2. *It was this person's intention to frame me for the murder **before** the murder actually took place.*

3. *Therefore, it is probably someone who knows us both.*

Motives

for killing Euphemia:

1. *To get revenge for something she did.*
2. *To frame me for something I did.*
3. *To keep her from revealing something.*

4. Because they ***think*** she did something, which may or may
not be true.

for framing me:

1. For gain. (Well, I do have a ***little*** put by. But Charles and
Belinda are the only beneficiaries.)
2. For revenge.
3. From jealousy.
4. To deflect suspicion from themselves.
5. Because they ***think*** I did something, which may or may not
be true.

She scratched away for several hours, with a goose quill pen
and violet ink. The notebooks were far too nice for the pencil
stub, unless she needed to write whilst away from home.

At half past ten o'clock, a supper tray was brought in, not
by Doyle or Mrs. Janks, but by Belinda herself, clad in her
nightcap and dressing gown and dressed for bed.

"Listen to this, Bunny," said Arabella, without looking up
from Euphemia's ledger:

> *"Z's farts smell of sosage and musterd,
> and he breaks wind freakently, so that
> you might think he was hard put to find
> a willing partner from among the stews.
> But he is a liberal client, likeing of
> variety, and I am ever amazed at the
> new praktizes he devizes for the
> enjoyment of the world's oldest amuse-
> ment. However, as frolicksum and
> inventive as he is with me, he only ever
> takes his wife from behind, as the sight
> of her face puts him right out of the
> mude."*

They both roared at this for some time, and Belinda, wiping her eyes at last, said, "It's good to hear you laugh again, Bell." She took the ledger from her sister, in order to appreciate Euphemia's inventive spellings.

"Well," said Arabella, "one cannot be grim *all* the time. On the other hand, laughing is not going to solve this case. Chances are, the murderer has already removed the page which bore his name."

"But why should he tear out so many?" asked Belinda, studying the book. "There are more stubs than pages, and they aren't even all together. Look, here's a clump of stubs, then there are three pages, two more stubs, another few pages, and then nothing but stubs to the end! Do you suppose his name was listed that many times?"

"I don't know. It's certainly strange. Well, as I cannot question people who are not listed, I shall have to see what can be done with the ones who are left. I have them written here, in my case notebook," she said, holding it up. "Do you like it?"

Belinda was enchanted. "It's lovely, Bell! May I carry it for you sometimes? It just exactly matches my new frock."

At the words "new frock," Arabella recollected herself.

"Forgive me, dearest! I was so wrapped up in my own affairs I never thought to ask how your shopping went! Did you get lots of nice things?"

"Not so many as Constance. She quite frightens me sometimes. Everyone knows the wench hasn't a penny, and she is always whining about how poor she is, yet she continues to rack up more debt every day."

"Yes, but not you."

"No, well, I remember what you told me, and I am always careful to stay within my budget."

"Good. Because, at the moment, *you* haven't got a penny, either."

"Bell," said Belinda, suddenly serious, "what will happen

to us? Now that the duke has withdrawn his patronage? How shall we live?"

"On credit, for the moment. But don't worry; I am in no doubt of finding another rich lover in the fall, when the *ton* come flocking back like the geese they so resemble."

"But what shall we do years from now? When you are old and debt ridden?"

(Belinda was only a few years younger than her sister, yet her mind was so constructed that it could not imagine a time when she might cease to be dependent upon Arabella, nor could she believe that her *own* face would ever lose its current appearance of fresh, dewy innocence.)

"You must not trouble yourself about such things," said Arabella indulgently. "For you will waste your youth if you do. Well, go on, then . . . tell me what you bought today."

"The blue frock, and a new bonnet for Sundays—"

"For Sundays?"

"In case I ever go to church."

"Why should you want to do that?"

"Well, in case I ever marry, you know."

Arabella smiled. "What, will you be married in a bonnet? In my day, brides used to wear orange blossoms and a veil."

"Oh! You're right, Bell! I never thought . . . but it's a nice bonnet all the same, and I daresay I shall find other occasions to wear it."

"Yes, I daresay you will," said Arabella. "Was that all you bought? A frock and a bonnet?"

"And this!" cried Belinda. She opened her dressing gown to reveal herself in a new nightdress, which was all over pink satin ribbons and lace, with little, embroidered roses.

"Oh, very pretty! You see? Shopping helps when you're feeling unhappy."

Belinda had recently lost her lover, a dashing young captain in the Grenadier Guards, who'd gone off and married an heiress. The poor child had been distraught at the time, and Arabella, seeking to console her, had said, "Marriage is an occupational hazard in this business. We courtesans cannot afford to become too much attached to our clients."

"Yes. That is, no, I know that," sniffled Belinda, with streaming eyes, "but I had been so *sure,* I mean I had hoped that he was going to ask *me* to marry him."

Arabella, who had been patting her sister's back and rocking her gently, now held her out at arm's length and looked her in the face.

"Belinda, darling, no man of property is just going to suddenly propose to you. You're not some virtuous little maiden with fifty thousand a year: You are a courtesan, and you have no money, other than what I can scrape together and whatever you are able to earn for yourself.

"If you wish to be married, and lead a dull, respectable life—although it's too late for us, you know, to ever be entirely respectable—we will need to plan it out first, very deliberately. I say 'we' because you will certainly need my help. But you must be very sure that that is something you actually *want,* dear. I don't believe that it is. I think you would be bored. And you would not be able to know *me* anymore, once you were married."

"I know that. But . . . but I want babies, Bell. And a house of my own."

"And a husband?"

"Yes. That, too."

"All right. Well, you go out and bury your bits when you're ready to, and come and tell me when you've completely got over the captain. Then, I promise, I shall begin to see about it."

Belinda was in the habit of retaining odd bits of trash that her lover of the moment had used or touched or that had once formed a part of his person: buttons, nail parings, shrimp shells from dinner . . . nothing was too insignificant or too disgusting. She had once claimed a soiled handkerchief into which her swain had expelled the gross side effects of his head cold, and her sister had expressed concern lest Belinda start asking her gentlemen friends to urinate into jam jars.

She kept these treasures in her bedroom, in an elaborate box that she had decorated herself, and then, after the affair inevitably ended, and Belinda inevitably recovered, she would take it outside and bury it in the garden.

"I shall miss your company, and your boxes, when you're married, Bunny," said Arabella gently.

"Oh, so shall I!" Belinda had wailed, and thereupon commenced a fresh round of weeping.

But that had been nearly two weeks ago, and now she had a new nightdress, which would invariably require a male admirer. Her broken heart was on the mend.

"Listen, Bell," she said. "This investigation of yours is terribly important to both of us. So perhaps we should cancel my birthday party."

Arabella was horrified. "Heavens no! With Uncle Selwyn coming? I couldn't think of it! Neddy and Eddie would be crushed if their first-ever grown-up party were canceled, to say nothing of you, darling . . . twenty years old and no party? Life mustn't come to a standstill, you know, merely because I have been inconvenienced!"

After Belinda had gone happily off to bed, Arabella went into her own bedroom, opened the drawer of her night table, and stood for some moments, holding the little bottle that she kept there. It had been immensely helpful, especially on nights like this one when she was too wound up to sleep. But she recalled Euphemia's neighbor with the itchy arms and the lice-ridden room. A woman who, though not old, had used up her life and would in all probability be as dead as Euphemia in a short time. Of course, Arabella might be, too. But if so, at least she would go to her grave as handsome and proud as she was at this moment.

She hurled the bottle from her window and watched it vanish into the darkness.

Chapter 8

A Case of Nerves

In which the thief is discovered, Arabella briefly loses her temper, a proposed dish is rejected, the servants are revealed as real people, Mr. Kendrick brings disappointing news, and Belinda proves incapable of telling one end of a horse from the other.

"Miss Beaumont! Madam! Some information for you, at last!" cried the chambermaid, sweeping into the bedroom and placing her mistress's tea tray on the nightstand.

Arabella was fully awake in an instant.

"Excellent, Doyle! What have you found out?"

"I wouldn't be knowin', ma'am, but Cook said I was to tell you it's important!"

Arabella hurried into her dressing gown. "Has my sister been informed?"

"Yes!" shrieked Belinda, bursting into the bedroom. "Here I am, Bell! Come quickly! Hurry! *Hurry!*"

But Arabella had to dash to the boudoir first, to retrieve her notebook. Then the Beaumont sisters flew down the stairs and tumbled into the kitchen.

Mrs. Molyneux, who had been rolling out a pastry crust, wiped her hands upon her apron and sat down at the big table, opposite her avid audience. The story, which concerned a sailor who'd stolen the paper knife (so there *had* been a sailor!), was actually quite sensational stuff. But to spare my readers from the tedium of Mrs. Moly's accent, the following précis is provided:

Cook's friend, a poulterer, told her of an occurrence recently related to him by his brother, who kept a tavern. Early in the previous week, a sailor who usually had no money had swaggered in, and before the tavern keeper could throw him out again the man had suddenly produced a wad of cash the size of a sandwich.

The sailor explained that he'd done an "inside job" for a gentleman who paid him a handsome price to obtain a trifling object. He'd been told to get one of her knives. "Which type?" the sailor had asked. "A carving knife? Bread knife? Cleaver?" "It doesn't matter which kind," came the reply, "just make sure it's sharp, and has her initials on it."

"I ask heem wheech night thees was, whan thee sailor cam into hees brother's tavern," said the cook, "and I mad heem work it out. Eet was the night after your own knife was stolen!"

Arabella fell back against her chair with relief, for now she knew that it had definitely not been her brother: Charles would not have had the money to bribe the sailor. Or, if Charles *had*, he would have figured out a way to *not* pay it. She fetched a quill and a bottle of ink from the breakfast room.

"So," she concluded, opening her notebook, and dipping her quill, "it was someone who knew me well enough to know that my silver is monogrammed!"

"Not necessarily," said Belinda. "Remember that article that ran about you in *La Belle Assemblée*? The one describing your daily life at Lustings? That mentioned the monogrammed silver."

"It did?"

"Yes," said Belinda.

"Hmm. What else do we have?"

"The sailor said it was harder than he'd expected, because

there were always people in the dining room," Belinda quoted, catching the cook's nod of approval. For Mrs. Molyneux's story had included more details than I have paraphrased above.

"Yes," said Arabella. "But then . . ."

". . . he found a paper knife on the desk in the library," Belinda repeated, "so he took that."

"But this is our man, surely!" cried Arabella. "Where is the sailor now, Mrs. Moly? Did the poulterer say?"

"*Non, madame.* But the tavern keeper might know."

"Good. I shall send a note to Mr. Kendrick, asking him to call upon this tavern keeper. He will be delighted at my assigning him a task. Come on, Bunny; let us have something to eat."

In the breakfast room, Arabella opened her secretary, for she planned to sit at the desk and write whilst she ate, but a ridiculous number of tiny, gaily wrapped packages spilled out onto the carpet.

"Goodness! I nearly forgot! Happy birthday, Belinda, dear! Here are some small gifts you may open now. There are more, upstairs, but I think that we shall save those for the party." (The princess having already laid claim to Belinda that night, the party would not be held for another two days.) "One would think she *might* have allowed you to spend your birthday with your family!" grumbled Arabella.

"Yes, but this way I get *two* parties," said Belinda. "Besides, you will have two more days in which to work up your case whilst it's fresh."

And as her sister happily unwrapped and exclaimed over each little bauble, Arabella simultaneously drank her coffee, penned a note to the Reverend Kendrick, and read the newspaper.

"Ha! Listen to this, Bunny:

"Durwent Frobisher, better known to his friends as 'The Beast,' has sired a child and married its mother, in that order. His bride, the former Harriet 'Heart of Stone' Hartley, has decided to name their daughter Lettice. Thus, into the annals of natural science are new inroads paved: the animal has married the mineral and quickly produced a vegetable.

"Do you not find that excessively diverting?"

"Who wrote it?" asked Belinda, holding out her arm to admire the new jonquil-colored glove with which she had just adorned it.

"Oliver Wedge. You remember—the editor we met at the auction."

"Mmm," said Belinda, removing the glove and reaching for another present. "Are you in love with him?"

When Belinda asked her this, Arabella had only just set down her coffee cup. Otherwise, she might have spluttered it all over the table. As it was, she only made a kind of protesting noise, there being nothing in her mouth *to* splutter.

"I cannot afford to fall in love, Bunny. It would be fatal to my business."

"Oho! It's the people who say they cannot fall in love who fall hardest of all!"

"I have not said that I cannot fall in love, only that I cannot *afford* to. I never have, though."

"I wonder why?"

"You see . . ." (And Arabella, having entered her instructional frame of mind, began waving her finger about in what Belinda privately held to be a most comical manner.) "It does not take very much to fetch most women. The majority of our sex are satisfied with good looks, political power, money, a title, or stamina, perhaps. But I require something more."

"And what is that?"

"I haven't the faintest idea. But in the meantime, I am perfectly happy to indulge in dalliances."

Arabella picked up the paper again.

"Is that *The Tattle-Tale*?" asked Belinda.

"It is."

"You have never wanted to read that one before. What was it you called it? 'A scurrilous rag'? Why have you suddenly begun to take it?"

Arabella blushed. "Well, I . . ." She cleared her throat. "Mr. Wedge has promised to help clear my name, if he can. It . . . they . . . his articles, I mean . . . will shortly be about me, once I grant him an interview. And I wanted to see what sort of writer he is."

"An interview? Bell, are you certain that this idea is a sound one? You know what journalists are like! Remember that cove from *The Daily Dispatch,* who nearly got you transported?"

Arabella had returned to her paper. "Pray, do not exaggerate, Bunny dear," she murmured. "Your integrity will develop premature wrinkles." A few moments passed. Then . . . "*Oh!* Of all the underhanded, inexcusable, dastardly tricks!"

"What?"

"Listen! Just *listen* to what he has written!

> " 'Tis a fine thing, indeed, when politicians turn deaf ears to desperately-needed social reform; when grave robbers, unchecked, tear our loved ones from their tombs, and when a murderess with high connections stalks the land, seeking her next victim!"

"Are you quite certain that he is referring to you?"

"Of course I am!"

"But he paid you such courteous attentions yesterday! The fellow was all affability, I thought!"

"I thought so, too," said Arabella. She sighed. "Well, Mr. Kendrick did warn me. He said Mr. Wedge was only out for a sensational story."

"Yes, but that man was attracted to you, Bell. I can always tell these things."

"Attracted or not, he's apparently out to crucify me."

"Well, perhaps it's fortunate that you have discovered his actual intent before granting him an interview. Now you can forget about that."

"Not at all! I fully intend to keep my rendezvous with Mr. Wedge."

"Oh, no, Arabella! Please don't! If there is anyone in the kingdom who can make your case weaker than it already is, Mr. Widgeon is that man. I fear it is his intention to render you a major disservice!"

"Well, he is going to be surprised then, because I intend to make mincemeat of *him!*"

Having thus dispensed with *The Tattle-Tale,* Arabella turned her attention to the post. There was an awful lot of it—condolences were pouring in from the members of her salon, and Belinda had to help her to open and read them all.

"Goodness, Bell," said she. "I believe this collection of letters from the great literary and scientific men of our time could form the basis of a book! It might be of great interest to posterity!"

"You are so delightfully silly, Belinda! It is one of the many things that I love about you. Consider, dear, whether the descendants of . . . Louis Trilby, for example, should like it known that their mighty ancestor was close friends with a courtesan!"

"I don't see why not . . . you are just as famous as he is!"

"Yes, but don't you see? His descendants are very likely to

be less so. And, being nobodies, they will elevate his stature in their own minds to be on par with God's, in order that they may bask in his borrowed light. They would therefore suppress such a book as mine, with threats of lawsuits and I don't know what all."

Arabella picked up an odd-looking envelope from the letter tray. It was addressed to her in an unfamiliar and childish hand, as though written by someone recovering from a stroke.

"Well, they cannot suppress a book that was published before they were born," said Belinda logically. "And you will have been dead for years before they would even be old enough to try it! That has to be one of the stupidest arguments I have ever heard you make, Bell. The truth is, you are just too lazy to gather these letters together and write the introduction!"

"Too *busy,* more like," said Arabella, absently slitting open the envelope. (She was using her new paper knife. On whose handle her initials *did not* appear.) "Besides," she said, "has it ever occurred to you that some of our friends may not want . . ." She trailed off as her eye traveled down the page. "Hmm. Listen to this, Bunny:

"Are you wurried about hangin'? Don't be. You will never hang as I am going to kill you first and when I do you will wish you was hangin' instede. I killed the first one fast, but you I shall kill slow. Your frend, anonimus for now."

Belinda was horrified. "How dreadful! You are in danger, Bell!"

"Oh, I don't think so. The constables are guarding me, after all. But it may be a clew, anyway."

"A clew! It's a threat! We must get away from here!"

"But where would we go? I am not allowed to leave London."

"Aren't you even the least bit upset?"

"Of course I am. I cannot make out this handwriting and it is obviously someone who knows me."

"If you knew them you would recognize the hand, surely."

"No, look," said Arabella. She took her pencil in her left hand and wrote "Your frend, anonimus" on the envelope. Then she compared the scripts.

"Why," said Belinda, "that is . . . singular. If Constance were here, she would say that you had written the letter yourself!"

Arabella smiled. "Do you see what it means, Bunny?"

"I must confess that I do not."

"Our 'anonimus frend' was writing with its other hand."

Belinda rubbed her thumb against her first two fingers to dislodge the crumbs and dabbed her lips with a flowered napkin.

"Perhaps," she said, "it's just some madman or -woman, stirred up by the murder."

Arabella snorted.

"Of course it isn't! Madmen aren't allowed to run about Brompton Park, threatening law-abiding citizens! They're properly locked up, and looked after . . . more or less."

"Why, that's so, isn't it? Constance told me that she recently went out to Bedlam with a large party, where for tuppence a head they were allowed to teaze the inmates as much as they liked! What do you think of that?"

"I think it is amazing that Constance, once admitted there, was ever allowed to come out again," said Arabella, offering to pour Belinda another cup of tea and receiving a negative shake of the head. "My point, Bunny, is that no sane society permits its drunkards, drug addicts, and lunatics to wander about the streets, accosting decent citizens."

"I suppose that is true, at present," she said doubtfully.

"And so will it always be," asserted Arabella, rising from the table. "Any society which would allow the mentally incapacitated to harass the competent would no longer retain the right to call itself civilized."

One of Lustings's best features, according to its mistress, was a deep, first-floor loggia at the side of the house, walled in green granite and extending out over the ground floor. Three stone arches, supported on columns, lent it a distinctly monastic flavor, a theme that was borne out by the simple trestle table and low wooden chairs. Not much used in the colder seasons, the loggia made a cool haven in which to eat, or merely to sit, on very warm mornings and afternoons. Just now, Arabella and Mrs. Molyneux were having tea there, whilst reviewing the menu for Belinda's birthday dinner, which was to take place the following evening.

"It all sounds perfectly wonderful, Mrs. Moly," said Arabella, casting an approving eye down the list. "But I wonder whether you could add a few curry dishes?"

"Curries?"

"Yes. Can you make them?"

"I *can*. But you have nevair ask for thees before."

"And I probably never shall again. But Uncle Selwyn will be joining us, as you know, and I think he rather got to like the stuff in Ceylon."

"Oh!" exclaimed the cook, reaching for a cream bun. "So *that* ees why I nevaire 'eard of thees Selweens before. He leev far away."

"Yes. But his wife has died, and now he is returning to England. Uncle Selwyn wrote us often before you came to

Lustings, and long ago he used to come for visits when home on leave. But my aunt never did; never wrote, never saw us. It was sad, you know, because she was probably the closest thing we had to a mother, growing up."

The cook clucked in disapproval and patted Arabella's hand. "Because you and Mees Belinda make sex for money, and she was ashamed of that."

"I suppose so. But she never seemed that sort of person. She wasn't judgmental in the least. Well. I shall never know, now."

Here the reader may be forgiven for feeling slightly at sea. It was *not* usual practice for mistress and servant to console each other over coffee and cream buns, but Lustings was run along somewhat original lines. And in order to understand the unique bond that Arabella shared with her servants, it is necessary that you know something of their histories.

Charlotte Janks, the housekeeper, was comfortable, forty-ish, plump, and gray haired. She was just one of many candidates who had answered Arabella's advertisement, all of whom were attracted by the generous salary and not put off by the Misses Beaumont's profession. But Mrs. Janks had arrived with a black eye—a good-luck gift from her husband—and with shoe soles worn right through from having walked the thirty miles to London.

"Have you any housekeeping experience, Mrs. Janks?" Arabella had asked, on being informed that the woman had brought no references.

"Bless you, miss! I've been keeping house these last thirty years—raising my children to grow up clean, kind, and honest, and giving them a warm and loving home."

"Well, that is commendable, but you haven't had experience working for a master, have you?"

"I should say I have! Harry Janks is the worst master in England, if not in Europe! I've been ill-used, cheated on, lied to, and shamed to my very bones. Yet I always kept the children safe from him, miss, that I did, and every one of them's gone out and done good in the world."

After the interview, Arabella told her, "I shall engage you, Mrs. Janks, on the sole condition that you leave your husband for good and promise neither to send him money nor to see him when he calls for you."

"Oh, but, madam! You don't know him! He's a monster when he's been drinking!"

"On the contrary, I know all I need to know of him. You needn't fear, Mrs. Janks; if your husband dares show his face here, my coachmen and gardeners will give him such a drubbing that it will permanently affect his memory."

"Ma'am?"

"I mean that he will forget entirely where you are living, and probably find himself some other poor woman to torture."

Arabella had first encountered her parlor maid, Marianne Fielding, whilst the latter was on trial for stealing a silver teaspoon, and facing deportation to Australia. Our heroine had been sitting in on the trial as a lark, watching her lawyer lover do what he did best. She had been touched by the girl's plight and volunteered to take charge of her after learning that Marianne had been desperate to raise money for her sister's abortion. People said she was mad to hire a maid who had already proven her untrustworthiness, but Arabella silenced the critics by asking, "What better punishment, then, than to be obliged to polish my silver teaspoons once a week for the rest of her life?"

"You are too good," the Reverend Kendrick had murmured. "If circumstances were different, you would be hailed as one of the greatest Christian philanthropists of the age."

Arabella had laughed. "Even though I never go to church?"

"Well, that's why I specified different circumstances."

"Oh! I thought you meant, if I weren't a wh—"

"Miss Beaumont, your carriage has arrived. Allow me to hand you in."

She had never had cause to regret her impulsive act. For Fielding, tall, serious, and all of nineteen years old, had proven herself to be a devoted and hardworking employee, and Arabella would have trusted her with the Star of India.

Little Sheila Doyle, Lustings's red-haired chambermaid, had been rescued by her mistress from Dublin's infamous Magdalene Laundry. Arabella had offered a certain sum to the mother superior, who, after praying about it, had happily informed Arabella that God had instructed her to take the money and release the girl. As mistress and servant were preparing to embark for London, however, word reached them that this same mother superior, Sheila's chief torturer whilst she was there, had died. Whereupon the girl had fallen to her knees and wept!

"Oh, madam! 'Tis my fault! Didn't I pray for the auld biddy to drop dead, and here she has! 'Tis a terrible sin I'm having on me soul now, for I've killed a bride of Christ!"

"Nonsense," Arabella had said, in her practical way. "*You* didn't kill that nun, Doyle; God killed her *for* you. Now get up, please, or we'll miss the boat."

Louisa Molyneux, or "Mrs. Molyneux," or "Cook," or "Mrs. Moly," was a refugee from the French Revolution. Arabella had played no part in her rescue; had, in fact, literally stolen her from the employ of Lady Ribbonhat. For on one occasion, when that august personage was vacationing in Biarritz, the duke had taken Arabella to the ancestral pile, and she had been so enchanted by the meals served to her there that she'd slipped into the kitchen and engaged this dark-haired, merry-eyed sylph on the spot.

Last, and, some might say least, was fourteen-year-old Tilda Crouch, who now helped Mrs. Moly in the kitchen. Crouch was illiterate and simple but good-hearted and anxious to please. The Misses Beaumont had found her one day, unconscious and starving on the streets, and had simply taken her home in their carriage.

In the beginning, Arabella's admirers, who were mostly men, with mostly ulterior motives, had occasionally tried to praise her for her Christian charity. But Arabella soon put a stop to that.

"Sow your field with wretches whom you've plucked from the depths," said she, "and reap a lifetime of faithful service for extremely low wages."

Of course, the wages she paid weren't really low. Quite the opposite, in fact, but her admirers weren't to know that. And when Arabella's servants had looked upon the rooms and beds that were to be theirs while they remained in her service, they were overcome with a gratitude so profound they could not speak.

She kept only women servants inside her house, but Arabella also employed male grooms and a coachman, who doubled as liveried butler and footmen; two gardeners; and a gardener's boy. These were all fine, lusty fellows—so Arabella made sure that they ate and slept in their own quarters, over the stables.

"Is that a horse I hear in the drive?" she asked, looking up from the menu. "Mrs. Moly, can you see who it is from over there?"

The cook stretched her torso out from under one of the loggia arches.

"Eet ees ze Reevrond Kendrick, madam," said she, nearly toppling down into the garden as she tried to retract herself.

"Excellent! Does he look pleased or perturbed?"

"I am sorry, madam; all I could see was hees-a horse's ass."

"Who's a horse's ass?" asked Belinda, emerging from the library.

"The Reverend Kendrick," said Arabella, absently scanning the menu once again.

"We could also 'ave ortolan," suggested the cook.

"What are those?" Belinda asked.

"Tiny songbirds, fattened on figs," Arabella replied. "No, I'm sorry, Mrs. Moly; there won't be time. We would have to special order them from France—there aren't any suppliers in Britain."

"Oh, but zere *are*, madame! An' we could easily catch zem ourselves! Zee birds in your aviatory are half-tame already! And zhust theenk of the wonderful feathers you would 'ave left over for trimming your 'ats!"

Arabella regarded her with horror. "Are you suggesting we should eat my Figpeckers?!"

"But av course! Not zhust ze Pigfuggers—*all* of your small bairds 'ave grown fat on a diet of fruit and delicacies. Zey would make delicious ortolan!"

"Mrs. Molyneux, you are not to consider such a thing! All sentiment aside, the aviatory's least expensive inhabitant cost me upward of ten pounds!"

"But 'ow can zat be?" cried the cook. "Whenever I go to feed zem, zey cry, 'Cheap! Cheap!' and I feel zat I am not making zee best use of your kitchen budget."

At this point, Arabella realized that the cook was cracking one of those monstrous Gallic jokes of hers. All the same . . .

"Mrs. Moly," she said, "I hereby absolve you from your bird-feeding duties. In future I shall assign that task to Tilda, exclusively." She suddenly noticed Belinda's presence. "Don't come out here, Bunny! You mustn't see what we're going to have until it's actually on the table!"

"But—"

"Go! *Go!*"

"All right, but do you *really* think that Reverend Kendrick is a horse's ass?"

"Belinda! How can you say such a thing? When he has always been so kind and considerate toward you!"

"But *I* didn't say that! *You* did!"

"Now you are not making sense! You aren't having a stroke, are you?"

Belinda began to cry.

Arabella was flabbergasted. "What in the world—What do you make of this, Mrs. Moly?"

"Eef she was having a stroke, I don' theenk she *could* cry."

Arabella rose and embraced her sister, patting her shoulder.

"All right. All right. There, there now, darling. I expect you're just suffering from pre-party excitement. Now you go inside where it's cool and have a little lie down. Ask Fielding to bring you a wet cloth for your brow."

"Good heavens! Whatever can be ailing Miss Belinda?" asked Kendrick in alarm, coming out onto the loggia. At sight of him, Belinda burst into a fresh spasm of weeping and hurried off to find solace elsewhere. Mrs. Molyneux went after her.

"It's the excitement," Arabella explained. "We are all on edge just now. Were you able to track down the sailor?"

"Yes and no. His name is Jack Furrow, but I am afraid you won't be able to talk to him; he sailed for Borneo shortly before the murder. In fact, that's probably why he was chosen to steal your knife, because his departure for foreign lands was imminent, and his likelihood of survival small."

"Mmm, yes," said Arabella reflectively. "He'll likely end up a titbit for cannibals. Well, at least we know that the murderer was a man, according to the sailor's testimony, someone who planned to implicate me *before* he killed Euphemia. That may or may not be significant."

She made a note in the blue notebook, which she had lately begun to keep with her when she went out and even when she stayed in, taking it along from room to room. Observing this, her thoughtful sister had netted her a bag for it.

After a bit, Belinda reappeared, looking somewhat more composed.

". . . So the murderer *definitely* wasn't Belinda," said Arabella, without looking up. A close observer might have seen a wicked little smile appear at one corner of her mouth.

"*What?!*" shrieked the poor child, hovering once again on the brink of hysteria.

"Oh, hush, darling; it was just in fun. I don't seem to be making much headway with this investigation, Mr. Kendrick."

"We mustn't give up hope, whatever happens."

"Why ever not?"

"Well . . . they taught us that in theological school," he explained uncomfortably. "But now I come to think of it, they never told us *why* we shouldn't. It is stupid, isn't it? Of course it must be all right to give up hope, once there can no longer be any point in clinging to it!"

Reverend Kendrick had never had any real affinity for the church. His family had thoughtfully arranged this career for him so that, as a third son, he mightn't starve to death. His one act of defiance had been in choosing the living at Effing, just so that he could make references, when he came into London, to "that Effing church! Those Effing choirboys!" He had also stubbornly refused to rise in the ranks. His grandmother had wanted him to become an archbishop, but she had died unfulfilled. In that respect, anyway.

"I mean, I'm not saying you should give up *now,* you know," he went on, wishing he could stop talking. "You haven't hit that brick wall yet. I'm sure there are still people you could talk to . . . or have me talk to. I should love to do something . . . anything I can! What are you . . . that is, how . . . do you know . . . ?"

"I have made an appointment to see an attorney," said

Arabella, "and then we shall see what we shall see. Will you stay to dinner, Mr. Kendrick?"

"Nothing would give me greater pleasure," he said. "But, as I am dining here tomorrow night, perhaps it would be better if I didn't."

He took courteous leave of both ladies and left them.

"It's just as well," muttered Belinda, on the point of blowing her nose. "He is rather a horse's ass, after all."

They were still laughing as Kendrick rode down the drive, and his heart warmed within his breast to think of the girlish merriment with which Arabella faced her uncertain future: Here was true courage, and unassailable nobility!

That night, over a game of whist with Constance, Belinda, and Mrs. Janks, Arabella, who couldn't keep her mind on the game, suddenly said, "The murderer *paid* a man to steal my paper knife. Then he used it to kill Euphemia. So he planned the whole thing out in advance. I think it is logical to assume that the murderer is someone known both to me and to Euphemia."

"Yes," murmured Belinda wearily. "So you've said."

"Arabella," said Constance slowly, and with the infinite patience of a madhouse attendant, "how can he possibly be known to Euphemia? She's dead."

"It might have been Puddles," said Arabella suddenly, turning from Constance and addressing herself exclusively to Belinda and Mrs. Janks. "With me out of the way, he could get his mother off his back, and reassure his fiancée. And there's that naval connection: The sailor might have been someone he knew from a previous voyage."

"But why should the duke want to murder Euphemia?" asked Mrs. Janks.

"Why should anyone? Maybe it was just so that he could frame me for it."

"No, Bell," said Belinda. "It cannot be the duke. He interceded to keep you out of gaol, after all."

"Well, that wasn't difficult to do; maybe it eased his conscience, which never pricks him very deeply in any case."

"But why should he hire someone to steal your paper knife," asked Constance, in a rare fit of common sense, "when he could have taken it himself during the party, or any time he was over here?"

"She's right, y'know," said Mrs. Janks. "It wouldn't make sense, involvin' a third party when he didn't have to. Besides, he was here with you on the night of the murder."

"If he paid someone to steal a knife, he might just as easily pay someone to do the killing."

"But why should he even *want* to?" Constance asked.

"Perhaps . . . his mother put him up to it."

"And why should she do that?" asked Belinda.

"This is what I have to find out."

Arabella got up from the table, picked up her volume of Lucretius, and settled herself in the window seat. "Just now," she added, "I am afraid that my own darling duke is the principal suspect."

Arabella's library was widely reputed to be one of the finest private collections of printed matter in the English-speaking world, but it certainly was not one of the largest. At a mere three thousand volumes or thereabouts, the books scarcely filled the room designated for the purpose of displaying and housing them. But each one had been especially chosen for its superior content, and each was an undisputed masterpiece of important ideas, of brilliant wit, of exceptional artwork, or of various combinations of these qualities.

She went through fads with her books. Just now, her favorite was *On the Nature of Things,* a poem in six volumes by Titus Lucretius Carus, a third-century Roman, whose work was widely credited with having inspired the Renaissance.

Arabella had recently decided that Lucretius's philosophy was the one she herself had been living for most of her life, i.e., that existence is transitory and therefore the only course that makes sense is the pursuit of pleasure and the avoidance of pain. This wasn't as selfish as it sounded, she argued, for it is not possible to live pleasurably without also being honorable, generous, kind, and courageous and without a genuine love for the other creatures that inhabit the earth. She thought it would be nice if everybody in the world read this poem or had it read to them. Failing that, she felt it her bounden duty to enlighten everyone whom she knew personally.

Nevertheless, when Arabella suddenly broke up the whist game in order to read Lucretius (to herself) yet again, Belinda was heard to remark that when the pursuit of one's own pleasure resulted in the termination of pleasure for others it was time to find a new book.

Belinda never was much of a scholar.

Chapter 9

THE DEVIL COMES TO LUSTINGS

*In which Mr. Wedge insults Lady Ribbonhat, Arabella
tells her story and attempts to play matchmaker, Neddy
brings his turtles, Mephistopheles arrives in time for
Belinda's birthday, and Euphemia gets laid . . . to rest.*

When Arabella arrived at the agreed-upon rendezvous
point in the formerly elegant section of Hyde Park
known as Vauxhall Gardens, she found Oliver Wedge there,
waiting for her. Of course she did; Arabella had arrived a full
quarter of an hour later than the time she herself had specified, for she intended to be the controlling force in this unac-
knowledged struggle that now existed between them. Wedge
wanted things from her, including information, and yet he had
printed an insulting, if not libelous, personal attack in his newspaper, which more than hinted at her guilt. It seemed to Arabella a most peculiar start to his promised assistance, and she
was angry . . . but also curious.

Wedge sat with one elegant leg thrown carelessly over the
other, his hat resting on his knee, with his gloves inside it,
and for a moment she imagined that he was not going to
bother standing up at all. He did, though, and made her a
courtly bow, which she returned with a cold nod.

"Miss Beaumont!" cried he, presumptuously taking her
hand and kissing it. "I was beginning to despair of you! I am
most awfully glad that you came!"

"I nearly didn't, you know," she replied icily. "After all your flattery and promises, to write such a thing in your paper . . . I must confess, I fail to understand your design."

"I am sincerely sorry, if I have given you pain—"

"*If!*"

"Yes, you see, the inspiration came to me in the wee hours, and there was no time to notify you of my idea before the morning edition. Not without sending an express post and waking you from your slumbers, which are surely of the utmost importance to your fresh-looking complexion and ethereal beauty."

"Enough of that, if you please. I find you both despicable and undeserving, Mr. Wedge, but should you care to oblige me with a recitation of this plan, I should be willing to listen to you for exactly five minutes."

"Shall we walk?"

He offered his arm, and Arabella hesitated a moment but took it.

"I think," said he, "that I shall begin my campaign—the newspaper campaign, that is—by vilifying you, and then gradually shift over to championing your cause. In that way, the reading public will think that they, too, have slowly come to realize how innocent you are, and how corrupt and incompetent the constabulary is."

"Really? Do you think it will work?"

"Madam, I *know* that it will. I have made it my life's employment to study the tastes and attitudes of London's citizens, and on your behalf I propose to cook up the public such a feast as it has never dreamt of. Am I forgiven?"

"I suppose so."

"Good," he said, and smiled. "We Catholics place a lot of importance upon that concept."

"You're a Catholic?" she asked.

"Is the Pope?" he rejoined. "I am *Irish*. I have no *choice*."

Arabella was thrilled to her toes. An Irish Catholic! A punch in the eye of English respectability! The ultimate in rebel chic! Here was a bad boy to her bad girl. They were made for each other.

Wedge paused to remove a small pocket book and pencil from his jacket, and Arabella was obliged to let go his arm whilst he did this. It vexed her to let go of him, and she noticed she was vexed.

"Miss Beaumont," said Wedge, "would you mind sharing with me your thoughts pertaining to society women—the so-called 'respectable' women—and how their position relates to that of courtesans like yourself?"

"I should be happy to, provided I have your assurance that you won't be using the information to denounce me."

"You have my word of honor upon it. I shall not be using this conversation at all until I have wholly taken up my stance in your favor. Publicly, that is. Privately, as I am sure you realize, you already have my complete and ardent admiration."

"How nice. To answer your question, Mr. Wedge, there is no difference between the two types of women, except that the courtesan is honest about what she does, and the respectable lady is not. In our society, a wife is nothing but a sort of domestic pet, with whom one has sexual relations. That this fact should be the source of her claiming superiority over the ladies of the night, who are free to love where they will and who call no man master, is absurd. But I am not complaining; we courtesans owe our very existence to the prejudice and inhibitions of respectable ladies."

"How so?" Wedge inquired, with genuine interest.

"It is their refusal to take pleasure in the gratification of their husbands' needs that drives their men to seek our company. If *all* women acted like whores, Mr. Wedge, there wouldn't be any."

"Women?"

"Whores!"

"Trollop!"

Julia van Diggle had chosen that moment to pass by with her prospective mother-in-law and had drawn a personal and unflattering inference from this last remark of Arabella's.

"Don't lower yourself to her level, Julia," admonished Lady Ribbonhat, staring straight ahead and slightly above the bridge of her own nose. "After all, *you* are about to become a duchess, and *I* am about to reclaim Lustings!"

"At your time of life, Lady Ribbonhat?" Wedge inquired severely. "I should be ashamed to own as much, were I in your place!"

"You should be ashamed in *any* case, sir, to be seen in company with that strumpet . . . !"

"I think I prefer 'trollop,' " Arabella murmured.

". . . and sitting by idly, whilst she insults her betters!"

"Her betters?" asked Wedge mildly. "Her betters do not live upon this earth, madam. Miss Beaumont is the most accomplished, the most brilliant, most wholly remarkable woman of her generation. But perhaps, not being a member of her generation yourself, you are unaware of this fact. If that is the case, I deem it an honor to have been the one to enlighten you."

He tipped his hat, put away his pocket book, and turned to Arabella, once again offering his arm. "Come away, Miss Beaumont. I fear the air, here, will do you but little good."

One may only imagine the state of high dudgeon in which they left the ladies, because at this point the two parties followed different paths, in opposite directions. And, since I have decided to follow Arabella and Mr. Wedge, I can tell you nothing of what was looked or done or said by the other pair.

The Tattle-Tale, like most of London's many periodicals, had its office situated on Fleet Street. The staff had recently removed to this location from a smaller office down the road, and the paper was doing very well here. For, as Oliver Wedge had more than once observed to his colleagues, "scandal sells."

"Have you seen the inside of a printing office before?" asked Wedge.

"Never," Arabella replied, gazing about her at the great presses and rollers and handsome copy boys, with sleeves rolled up over their well-turned, muscular forearms, "though I've been in print *shops* of course. I am one of Ackerman's regular customers."

"I am sure you are. Well, we don't produce art prints here . . . yet, but we don't just print newspapers, either. I also publish books. Only limited editions for now, but one day I hope to expand that side of things." He took her arm protectively, conducting her past the leering copyists and typesetters and printers and journalists. "I expect this office will look very different in a couple of years, once they have perfected the steam printer."

"Why?" asked Arabella. "What will those look like?"

"I don't really know, but I intend to get one the moment they're available. Supposedly, they will make it possible to increase our output tenfold. Right now, each of my presses prints two hundred sheets per hour. Imagine one that could turn out eleven hundred! This is my office," he said, opening the door. "We shan't be disturbed in here."

Arabella took the proffered seat, and Wedge sat, not behind his desk but opposite her, placing his chair very close to her own. "The more London knows about Arabella the woman, as opposed to Arabella the courtesan," he explained, "the more it will pity your plight, and fight to save you. Your salvation, Miss Beaumont, lies with *The Tattle-Tale*'s readers. Please, won't you tell me your story?"

Arabella decided to oblige him, for she guessed that he

would find it interesting. And doubtless the reader of this book will, too.

The Beaumont siblings—Arabella, her older brother, Charles, and her younger sister, Belinda—were the children of a baronet and his wife, a squabbling pair of Georgian roués and close friends of William Beckford's, if not of each other. This precious pair gambled and gamboled, perpetrating scandals, staging monumental rows in public, losing prodigious sums at the gaming table, and ruining their constitutions, to say nothing of their bank account, until both were quite played out.

Before that happened, though, their relentless pursuits of pleasure leaving them time for little else, they left the raising of their three children to nursemaids. And if there is one thing that argues in favor of being brought up by nursemaids (though it is doubtful that there could be more than one thing) it is that it gives one the chance to be completely objective about one's parents. Arabella soon found that she detested hers.

Lord, what *awful* people, she thought to herself when she was five. And inwardly she resolved to have as little to do with them as possible. But children do not grow up in vacuums, and Arabella had developed a passionate attachment to her nursemaid, Molly. So when that sweet-natured young woman died, suddenly, of an inflammation of the lungs, Arabella considered herself an orphan, even though both her parents were at that time still alive and kicking. And hitting. And, in at least one notable instance, biting.

When at long last they did die, they left nothing behind but the family manse. This went to Charles, of course, and he promptly lost it at cards.

Charles and Belinda were both uncommonly attractive specimens, but without the favor of fortune neither could hope to marry well. And Arabella, practical though she was, refused to entertain the thought of marrying at all. So when the cost of her parents' funerals used up the money realized from the sale of the family carriage, the Beaumonts were faced with almost certain starvation.

Fortunately, Lady Beaumont's funeral had been attended by the notorious Fortescue sisters, first cousins to the orphaned Beaumonts, and whilst the son used his mother's death as an excuse for a drinking binge, Amber, Ivy, and Claire had whisked her daughters off to a party. The girls had a wonderful time and were eventually inducted into the family establishment, where they learnt all manner of pleasing arts. There they might have remained indefinitely, but for the lucky chance of Arabella's capturing the heart of the Duke of Glen*deen*. She had toyed with it for a time, but now he had withdrawn that organ from her, in order to make a formal presentation of it to Julia van Diggle.

". . . and that is my story, Mr. Wedge."

"Very compelling, too," he said, glancing up from his tablet and fixing her with his admiring and therefore seductive eyes. They were the color of malt whiskey. Rather than inspiring Arabella with Dutch courage, though, they filled her with a kind of panic. She held his gaze just long enough for convention's sake, with slightly raised eyebrows and a cool, ironic smile. Then she shifted her eyes to the painting that hung on the wall behind him, Wedge's own portrait.

"That's a Thomas Lawrence, is it not?" she asked, being too far away to read the signature.

"It is," said Wedge. "And it cost me a pretty penny! Or it will, when I've paid for it. But that doesn't matter, because, you see, I am planning a newspaper empire that will eventually become powerful enough to change the course of world events. When that happens, years from now, this portrait will hang in the conference room of an enormous commercial building."

"Hmm," said Arabella. "It isn't like you, somehow, and Lawrence is usually very true to his subjects."

"His portraits of the Prince of Wales aren't like *him*, either."

"No—that's flattery. This doesn't make you look better. Just *different*. It's crooked, too."

She rose and crossed to the portrait, to straighten it.

"Be careful of the canvas," cautioned Wedge. "The paint's not dry yet."

Arabella stood for a moment, gazing up at the picture that was and was not like Oliver Wedge. It was odd.

"Bell?" called Belinda up the stairwell. "Neddy and Eddie are here!"

Half siblings Edward and Edwardina, the unlawful progeny of Charles Edward Beaumont, stood in the foyer amidst a profusion of toys, portmanteaus, tennis racquets, and mothers. Arabella paused at the top of her curving staircase in order to fully appreciate the scene, which reminded her of a setting for one of Mr. Gillray's cartoons.

The children looked nothing like their parents, yet both resembled each other a good deal: white skinned and rather sickly, with pale, flat hair and colorless eyes. Eddie had potential, though. Girls like this, provided they survived past adolescence, often grew into stunning beauties. Boys, on the other hand, tended to remain as they were, only larger.

Neddy was pink and swollen around the eyes and nose today and on this account looked something like a white rat—a white rat holding a large box in front of it and emitting loud, wet sniffles at regular intervals. Evidently, he had recently thrown one of his signature tantrums.

"Here you are at last, my dears!" cried Arabella, pretending to be glad.

Edwardina made her a fine little curtsy, but the churlish Neddy merely fixed her with a pink-rimmed, sullen glare.

"Neddy's sulking," said his mother. "Pay no attention to him."

Polly was a hardworking, somewhat hard-boiled young courtesan, who had little patience with her whining son, while Sarah-Jane, Eddie's mother, had nothing but goose down where her brains should have been.

"What have you there, Neddy?" asked Arabella. "May I see?"

The child continued to glower, without answering, so she removed the lid herself, and they both peered in at the contents.

"Oh! What lovely turtles! What have you named them?"

"Klunk and Stupid Looking. That turtle is Klunk and that turtle is Stupid Looking," said Neddy, pointing.

Why was it that children generally took so long to master the pronoun?

"Klunk?" said Belinda, wrinkling her nose. "That's a funny name! Whatever does it mean?"

"Doesn't mean anything," the boy replied, sticking out his lower lip. "That's the sound he makes when I kick him downstairs!"

"You mustn't do that, Neddy," said Belinda seriously. "It's cruel, and you could break his shell that way."

"Good!"

"Why have you given these wonderful creatures such hateful names?" asked Arabella.

"Because," the child replied, raising his voice, "I wanted a *puppy!*"

"As if I hadn't enough to do without housetraining a puppy!" Polly explained. "I shall observe his interactions with the turtles and review the matter again. But based on what I have seen so far, I very much doubt that we shall be getting a dog."

She addressed herself chiefly to Belinda, as Arabella had

already grown bored with the conversation and seemed scarcely to be listening.

"Polly," she said, glancing out the window, "did you notice the Bow Street Runners standing guard in front of my house?"

"Yes. They must be a great vexation to you!"

"Oh, not so much. What do *you* think of them, Sarah-Jane?"

"The dark one is awfully handsome!"

"Really? Actually, I had him in mind for Polly. Could you like the fair one?"

Sarah-Jane shrugged. "I prefer my men dark," she said. "Always have done."

"What do you say, Polly?"

"I wonder why you are asking these questions," said Polly crossly. "What you do with your time is your own business, but I want it known here and now that I have no intention of participating in any of your drunken debauches!"

"Heavens! You mistake me!" cried Arabella. "I was just thinking how nice it would be if Neddy and Eddie were to have real fathers."

For if they had, thought she, their mothers could stay at home and take care of them properly and they wouldn't always need to be coming out to Lustings. (Arabella sometimes engaged in altruistic schemes, but this was not one of them.)

Once the children were settled in, their mothers left and their aunties took them onto the roof, where the telescope was. The views were splendid from up there, and a little promenade fence round the perimeter kept people from falling off.

Neddy generally tried to spy into other people's windows, but Eddie always looked down at the roads. Neither child was interested in the heavens.

"What can you see?" asked Belinda of her niece, who was squinting through the eyepiece.

"A coach!" she said excitedly. "It looks like a post chaise, and it is headed this way! It's simply *crowded* with trunks and things!"

"How do you know it's a post chaise?" Neddy sneered. "You couldn't possibly read the door from this far away. It's probably a private carriage!"

"I said it *looks* like one," said Edwardina. "It's yellow, it's got luggage on top, and it's going very fast. Besides, why should anyone with a private carriage want to paint it to *look* like a post chaise?"

Eddie had promised her mother not to squabble with Neddy, but why did he always have to be so disagreeable?

"Here," he said, suddenly shoving her out of the way. "Let *me* look!"

"*Ow!*" she cried, for Neddy had knocked her against the telescope, nearly upsetting it, and injuring her elbow.

Arabella would not stand for this. She pushed her nephew suddenly in the chest, propelling him violently backward.

"No," she said. "*I* am going to look, because it's *my* telescope, and I think that coach has my uncle inside it! You see?" she said to Neddy, who was rubbing his chest and looking aggrieved. "It hurts to be pushed around like a sack of turnips, doesn't it? Well-bred young ladies and gentlemen do not push one another; they wait their turn, like civilized persons."

"*You* pushed *me,*" he remarked rudely.

"Yes. Sometimes it is more effective to demonstrate a lesson than merely to talk about it. And I suspect you to be the type of child who learns best by doing, or, in this case, by being done to."

Belinda had taken advantage of the impromptu lesson to snatch a look through the telescope herself. "It *is* Uncle Selwyn," she pronounced, with satisfaction. "Let us go down and wait for him in the porte cochere!"

Arabella's porte cochere was a dual-purpose structure. It

was both a shelter where carriages could load and unload during inclement weather and a wonderful place to have tea. The roof was supported by eight Corinthian columns of Portland stone, with marble caryatids arranged between them. A table with collapsible legs and a set of folding chairs could be lowered from the ceiling at a moment's notice and set up to accommodate six persons.

The post chaise, for that is indeed what it was—Eddie stuck out her tongue at Neddy when no one was looking—pulled up easily beneath the loaded ceiling with room to spare and discharged its distinguished passenger.

The last time Arabella had seen him, Sir Geoffrey Selwyn had been an imposing, corpulent man, with a big, florid face. Now he was grown alarmingly spare and his complexion was a sickly gray. As Arabella's grooms came out to unload the equipage, His Lordship handed one of them a mysterious-looking dome-shaped parcel, swathed in Indian calico, which he had been nursing on his lap.

"Mind you be careful of that," he said. "It is Miss Belinda's birthday present!"

But as Trotter was taking hold of the object, a malevolent voice thundered out of it, and the coachman nearly dropped it in surprise. The sudden jolt apparently occasioned a stream of obscenities from within, articulated in a particularly nasty, insulting tone, and its hearers were thrilled with a kind of delighted horror.

"What have you there, Uncle? A Pygmy?" asked Arabella.

But Belinda knew what it was. "Oh!" she cried, her eyes sparkling with joy. "It's a parrot!"

When Sir Geoffrey's gear had been unloaded and carried off to the house, Arabella had the table and chairs brought down from the ceiling of the porte cochere and dismissed the children to play in the stream.

"May we take our shoes and stockings off?" asked Eddie,

her eyes nearly popping from her head with unbearable expectation.

"I insist that you do so," said their aunt. "You will ruin them, otherwise."

She turned to one of the Runners, who'd been standing a short distance away, trying to look inconspicuous. "Mr. Dysart, would you be so kind as to ask Cook to send us out some lemonade?"

"Good lord!" exclaimed her uncle, after the man had gone. "Was that a policeman?"

Briefly, Arabella outlined her situation.

"How dreadful for you, my dear!"

"I am attempting to solve the case on my own, Uncle," she said. "So if I must leave you to your own devices much of the time, I hope that you will forgive me."

"Of course you must do whatever is necessary to clear your name," said Sir Geoffrey, patting the hand of his other niece. "After all, I shall have your pretty sister here to keep me company."

"I may not be around much, either," said Belinda apologetically.

"Our Bunny has become the favorite of the Princess of Wales," said Arabella. "And is apt to be summoned to the royal presence at all hours."

Uncle Selwyn was astonished. "The Princess of Wales? Why ... I ... How amazing!"

"It is not what you think," said Belinda. "I haven't been miraculously restored to polite society or anything."

Arabella nodded. "You have been away many years, Uncle Selwyn. You probably don't know about the princess."

"She's half-mad," Belinda explained, "and goes about dressed in the most peculiar fashion—put a scooped-out melon on her head, once; said it made a very cool sort of hat. She frequently appears at fancy dress parties naked to the waist, claiming to be Venus, or Lady Godiva. She likes to be shocking. The prince regent keeps trying to divorce her, but the princess has very good lawyers. And, anyway, Parliament won't allow it."

"Upon my word!"

"The world is changing," said Arabella. "Or at least, society is."

"Yes. As you say," said Sir Geoffrey, "I have been away much too long. Got no connections here anymore, except for you two and Charles. And what with my own sweet Sophia gone from me now . . ." Here the dear old fellow pulled a handkerchief from his breast pocket and applied it to his eye corners. "I thought, you know . . ."

"Of course," said Arabella. "We welcome you with open arms, Uncle. My sister and I very much hope that you will decide to come live with us."

"Well!" he exclaimed. "That is very kind, and I am most obliged to you, but the fact is . . . that is, I . . . Oh, dash it all! Why should I hide the truth from *you?* I left my heart behind in England when I went off to Ceylon with your aunt, and the lady is a widow now. We've been . . . writing to one another for almost a year, and it is settled that I shall go and stay with her, until . . . well, until my health breaks down. I won't go into detail, but I am not long for this world."

Arabella patted him sympathetically on the shoulder. His news had not shocked her, for she had seen death in his face the moment he alighted from the carriage.

"Miranda—that is, Mrs. Ironmonger—and I plan to marry at once."

"Ironmonger!"

The cry of delighted disbelief had burst simultaneously from both of the Beaumont throats.

"Yes. It used to be 'Smith,' but her late husband had it legally changed, at her urging."

"Why?" asked Arabella. "Did she think 'Ironmonger' sounded more genteel?"

"No. It wasn't that way at all. Miranda . . . the lady . . . my friend used to get the queerest looks whenever she had to say or sign the name 'Smith' in any place where she was not known by sight. People thought she must be hiding some shameful secret, and giving a false name, as her real one should be instantly recognized. That never happens now, with 'Ironmonger.' "

"Well! This is splendid!" said Arabella.

"I think it's terribly sad!" sniffed Belinda, whose eyes had begun to leak.

"Yes, it's that, too," Arabella agreed. "Uncle Selwyn, I am so happy for you, and sorry for you, and sorry for us, that we shall be losing you so soon . . . but modern medicine has made great strides in the past ten years. You have not yet been to see a London specialist. Perhaps you are not so ill as you think."

He shook his head. "There is no hope, I have already looked into it. But I am old, you know, and quite resigned to it. As for Mrs. Ironmonger, she is nearly my age, and not very well herself. If I die first, I shall leave her comfortably well off, with the remainder of my estate going to you two and Charles. Mrs. Ironmonger has no family of her own, so she will leave everything to you, as well."

"All right, but for heaven's sake, do not breathe a word of this to Charles! He will come swooping in, demanding an advance on his inheritance, and then, given time, will bleed you both dry."

"Hm. Still addicted to gaming, is he?"

"That, and other things."

"Well, I shall certainly take steps to ensure Mrs. Ironmonger's financial safety. And also," he said, smiling and patting her arm, "yours and Belinda's."

When Mrs. Janks appeared with refreshments, Sir Geoffrey sent for the calico dome, observing with a practiced and appreciative eye the housekeeper's ample backside as it retreated across the lawn.

"We need to unwrap his cage as soon as possible," explained Sir Geoffrey. "Otherwise he becomes sullen. Goes off his food . . . won't do anything but swear, and I do want him to make a good first impression."

The dome was brought and placed before Belinda to unwrap. For some time past, she had wanted a parrot, the real talking kind, with brilliant feathers of gold and green and purple. So when she removed the cloth and saw only a bright-eyed black bird, with an orange beak and yellow ear lappets, she was visibly disappointed.

"This is Mephistopheles," said her uncle. "I've taken to calling him 'Fisto,' for short. What do you think of him?"

"He's very nice," said Belinda politely. "But I thought he was a parrot."

"Oh, a mynah bird is much *better* than a parrot, my dear. A parrot can only squawk in a harsh voice, and say a few very limited things. Watch this."

When the fresh air and sunshine touched him, Fisto ruffled his neck feathers and shook his head rapidly as if to clear it.

"Ahhh!" said the bird appreciatively. "That's *much* better!"

"Yes, you're happy now, aren't you, Fisto? Hey? This is Belinda. Do you remember what I taught you to say to her? Happy . . ."

"Happy birthday, Belinda, my dear! Many, many happy returns of the day!" said Fisto, in a perfect imitation of Sir Geoffrey's voice.

Belinda was enchanted.

"He's very cunning," said their uncle. "Fisto can repeat anything you say, in your exact *voice*. And listen to this!"

He dropped a teaspoon onto the table. The bird reproduced the sound exactly. "No parrot can do *that!*"

The girls were speechless with astonishment.

"Where should we put his cage?" asked Belinda, at last.

"Why not set him free in the aviatory?" Arabella suggested. "He would probably like that."

"I shouldn't advise the aviatory," said Sir Geoffrey. "He will imitate the other birds and fuss them. Fisto is much more stimulated—not to mention amusing—when he lives amongst people."

"Well, Bunny's a light sleeper," said Arabella. "So I shouldn't like to put him in her bedroom, but I suppose we might keep him in mine."

Her uncle shook his head, again. "I wouldn't, you know. Think what might happen if the bird were to call out a certain name, in your voice . . . when someone *else* is . . . visiting you."

"*Ho!* I begin to see why you named him 'Mephistopheles'!" she exclaimed, laughing. "That would be too awkward, would it not? Never fear; he shall stay in the breakfast room, and liven us up in the mornings."

It was Cook's night off. Sir Geoffrey, having apprised his friends some weeks earlier of his imminent return, was being feted that evening at his club, and Neddy and Eddie, under the care of Mrs. Janks, were attending a children's party. Arabella and Belinda were on their own.

"Sister mine, what would you say to burgundy and oysters with a nice, plump chop at Grillon's?"

"Ooh! Yes, please!"

"We shall go incognito, public sentiment being what it is."

"What is it?"

"Unpredictable."

In addition to their glamorous traditional wardrobes, courtesans generally kept a wide selection of theatrical costumes. For the tendency toward erotic obsession found in *Homo sapiens* so sets our species apart from every other that it may one day become determinative in gauging relative degrees of humanity in any yet-to-be-discovered intermediary primate groups.

On this particular night out, Arabella and Belinda easily disguised themselves with the aid of wigs, false eyebrows, and foreign clothing—creating an impression that they augmented by assuming Russian accents. All these precautions would have been in vain, however, had the sisters been seen in one of Arabella's distinctive carriages. So they walked out to the Brompton Road and Constable Dysart hailed them a cab.

"Why don't we simply walk to Grillon's?" Belinda asked.

"Because I want to stop someplace else, first. Do you mind?"

"I should have known there would be a catch."

"This won't take long, Bunny," said Arabella. "And it is something that I need to do."

The windows in the hired coach were open, for the evening air was cool after the heat of the day, almost as soft and fresh, on this particular evening in filthy old London, as it is every night of the year in the unspoilt English countryside. Arabella filled her lungs with the sweet-smelling atmosphere. "What an evening!" she exulted. For, ever since her near arrest earlier in the week, she had suddenly become much more observant and appreciative of her surroundings.

"Have you noticed, Bunny? The way everything seems to stand out sharply against the light of yesterday, like memories made more vivid when illuminated by the intensity of retrospection?"

"Bell," said Belinda after a moment. "I am glad that you have decided to embrace life after all, but I really don't think it can be healthy for you to be spending quite so much of your time with intellectuals."

A quarter of an hour later, the cab was obliged to halt for a massive procession: A hearse was making slow and stately progress along Fleet Street, followed by at least a hundred people shuffling silently in its wake and carrying torches. Less silent, but no less solemn, a veritable mob waited on both sides of the road to witness the funeral procession on its way to the churchyard at St. Bride's.

"Who gets buried at night?" Belinda wondered aloud, remembering to use her accent.

"Euphemia Ramsey," said Arabella quietly. For she had read about this in *The Tattle-Tale:* Euphemia had left particular instructions with regards to her interment, the expenses of which her impoverished estate was unable to meet. Fortunately, some of her former clients had stepped in, and the funeral was being handled by subscription.

"Is this why you've come here?"

"Yes," said Arabella quietly. "She used to be my friend, you know, and I cannot very well attend her funeral, suspected as I am. Farewell, Euphemia."

"Look, Bell!" said Belinda, pointing. "It's that odious Oscar Widgehunt!"

"Do you mean Oliver Wedge? I *do* wish you would stop mangling his name. Your feelings about him are perfectly clear. Where is he?"

"Over there, halfway up a lamppost, writing in a notebook," said Belinda, nodding in his general direction. "Mayn't we go to Grillon's now? I am hungry enough to eat the paving stones!"

At last their cab pulled into Albemarle Street, and when Arabella alighted and paid the driver he tipped his hat to her.

"God bless ya, Miss Beaumont," said he. "You won't be

disappointing yer public now, will you? We're all expectin' you to go out in style."

Suddenly the evening seemed a little less bright.

"So much for our disguises," said Belinda. "But at least he didn't try to tear you limb from limb."

"No," Arabella muttered. "You heard the man—he would rather wait and see me go out in style."

After the ladies had been seated, Oliver Wedge entered the restaurant with three cronies and took a table near the windows. The Beaumonts had decided to begin their meal with oysters, but Wedge's party dispensed with the formalities and immediately plunged into the main courses.

"That's strange," said Arabella.

"What is?"

"Mr. Wedge is eating beefsteak."

"There's nothing strange about that," said Belinda. "It's exactly what I am going to have."

"Yes, but today is Friday."

"So it is!"

". . . and he's a Catholic."

"Well, perhaps he isn't a very good one."

"No, indeed," she replied thoughtfully. "Not a very good one at all."

Chapter 10

A CLEAN BREAST

In which it may be seen that Constance is a thorough-going nuisance, Arabella has covert tendencies, and Runners make excellent child minders. A singular discovery comes to light via an unexpected source.

" 'Executioners are sometimes lent to other countries for important executions. They cost more, of course, but are definitely worth it for beheadings. For hangings, you are well advised to save your money and shew your patriotism by hiring a local man.' "

Arabella sighed. "Constance . . ."

" 'Last words, if tasteful, are expected and proper on such occasions. Keep your audience engaged: Be brief, and try to express remorse, forgiveness and good resolutions in under three minutes if you can.' "

"I say, Constance, would you mind not reading aloud from that?"
Belinda entered the library with a fruit bowl.

"Whatever is the matter?" she asked, observing the pained expression on her sister's countenance.

"I am very busy just now," replied Arabella crossly, "but Constance *will* insist upon lecturing me about the minutiae of gallows etiquette. Who let her up here?"

"It wasn't me. Perhaps it was Fielding."

> " 'As you pass from prison to gallows, the happy mob will accompany your cart and attempt to press drinks upon you. Accept their offerings freely, by all means, and toss back the empty cups with equal good humor. Witty remarks, though favored by crowds, are not within the capabilities of every condemned person. Just let them see that you are cheerful, and they will admire you for it.' "

"Hello, Constance," said Belinda. "Would you care for some grapes?"

"Ooh yes I adore them hello Belinda I've just come from Hookham's where I found this," she said, holding up her book with one hand and popping grapes into her mouth with the other. "You see? *Mr. Beaston's Proper Deportment for Condemned Persons*—it wasn't too expensive really not when you consider all the use we'll be making of it and I thought dear me this is just what poor Arabella needs because I didn't suppose she knew the first thing about what to do in a case like this none of her friends having been through it before so I nipped on over here quick as I could because it's never too soon to start educating oneself, is it? Listen to this:

> " 'Bodies of the hanged may either be displayed in some public place, or buried immediately, pre-

ferably at a crossroads. Sometimes, the condemned is given a choice, beforehand.' "

"Now I never knew that did you? I wonder if Arabella will
be given a choice."

"Bunny," said Arabella, "why don't you take Constance
out of doors? The garden is particularly lovely, just now."

"Come along, Constance," said Belinda, pulling Miss
Worthington by the elbow. "You can read to *me*—Bell has
important business to attend to."

But after they had gone, Arabella sucked the end of her
quill for a few moments and then flung it down in disgust:
Her concentration had fled, for the time being. She placed
her CIN into the bag that Belinda had made for it, sharpened
the pencil stub that she kept behind her ear, and began to
dress to go out. Today, she would wear white, to underscore
her innocence—in the murder of Euphemia, anyway—for she
was about to consult a lawyer, and Arabella wanted him on
her side. She stole a quick glance out of the window. If Constance should guess that Arabella was taking the carriage, she
would clamor to be dropped somewhere very much out of
the way or, worse, insist upon accompanying her friend, chat-
tering mindlessly for the duration of the journey and reading
aloud from that macabre book of hers.

However, Constance was fully engaged in reading to Belinda, who had taken her workbasket outside with her and
who now sat demurely upon the stone bench, listening, whilst
threading satin ribbons through a stack of sheep gut condoms. Arabella saw with satisfaction that Belinda was engaged on the medium-sized ones—which they were always
running out of—for she could see the silver ribbons from
where she stood. (The small ones had pink ribbons, large
ones gold, and the enormous-sized condoms had blue ribbons—like those awarded to first-prize stallions at horse

shows.) Though the two women were seated some distance from the house, Arabella could still hear Constance reading, with perfect clarity:

> " 'The custom of publically tipping the hangman moments before your execution is considered excessive and should not be encouraged. Make use of this occasion to shew your community a good example.' "

So . . . Constance and Belinda were out in the garden and Sir Geoffrey had taken Mrs. Ironmonger to view the Elgin marbles. If Arabella left now, no one would notice, except whichever Runner was assigned to her today, and he would be coming with her in any case.

Out in the carriage house, her foot upon the step . . .

"Aunt Bell, Aunt Bell! Where are you going? Mayn't we come, too?"

Damn! She'd forgotten about the children!

"Not this time, my dears; I have some calls to make, and you would be left in the landau, perhaps for hours. You would be very bored."

"No, we shouldn't! We should love it! Please! It's been ever so long since we've had an outing!"

This was untrue. They had only arrived yesterday. *That* had been an outing.

"No," said Arabella. "Now don't tease, or you won't be allowed to stay up for the party."

"In that case," said Neddy, "I shall go round to the garden, and let Miss Worthington know that your carriage is leaving."

"Don't do that, you little bugger!" (How had he divined that she particularly wanted to avoid Constance?)

"You must let us come with you, then."

She was trapped.

"Very well, Edward. But I would have you know that your conduct sits very ill with me. I shall remember this, and be inclined to do you a disservice one day in recompense."

"Not me, though," said Edwardina smugly, climbing in and settling next to her aunt. "I rape all of the benefits, and yet am not penisized."

"What was that you said?"

"The benefits. I rape them, but I am not penisized, as Neddy is."

"I think you mean that you 'reap' the benefits without being 'penalized.' "

"That's what I said. Oh, Aunt Bell, may we have the top down? *Please?*"

Landaus are uniquely constructed with two separate folding hoods, one at the front and one at the back. Usually, this means that the passengers may have either one up, or neither, or both, and the two hoods meet in the middle for total coverage. But just now there was something wrong with the mechanism. Trotter, who was tinkering with it in his spare time, had not quite resolved the problem yet, and for the time being one could only have both hoods down or both up. Arabella wanted both up today, for she was wearing white and London's filthy air would scarcely have enhanced her appearance. It was going to be infernally hot under the hood, but the children were not to be dissuaded on that account.

The carriage was just clearing the gate when a horrific stench hit it like a slap in the face.

"Faugh!" cried Arabella, holding her nose. "What *is* that, Trotter?"

It was some moments before her coachman was able to reply, plagued as he was with retching spasms.

"Dead horse, ma'am," he gasped.

"A dead horse? Next to my gate? Did you notice it there yesterday?"

"No, ma'am. And it's not a fresh one, if you'll pardon my saying so; been dead a week, at least."

"So someone has put it there, have they?"

"I would say so, ma'am, yes, partly on account of its ripeness, but also because of the sheep."

"Sheep?"

"The dead sheep on t'other side of the entrance, ma'am."

The carriage having moved on at once, Arabella could not now observe this, but the stench seemed to cling to the coach for some little ways.

"I smell Lady Ribbonhat," said the self-possessed Edwardina.

"Well, she reeks something *awful*," Edward rejoined.

"How do you know about Lady Ribbonhat?" asked Arabella.

"Oh, I know all about everything," said Eddie. "The murder charge and the duke's engagement to Miss van Diggle and everything."

"I did not ask you *what* you knew, but *how*."

"Because I listen, Aunt Bell. Grown people, ladies especially, think children are stupid, so they talk freely in front of us. But we aren't."

"You can always tell a lady," muttered Neddy, "but you cannot tell her much."

"Well, *some* of us are stupid," Eddie conceded, with a glance at her half brother, "but *I'm* certainly not."

"No," echoed her aunt faintly. "You certainly aren't."

Turning to look out the back window, Arabella saw both Frank *and* Tom, running along behind and coughing into their handkerchiefs. Generally, there was only one Runner at a time now, but both of them were on duty today, as the schedule at the Bow Street office had got muddled. Again.

Arabella was gratified to know that she was not the only one who was having a difficult day.

"I need to speak with you, Aunt Bell," said Neddy, "on a rather urgent matter."

"I see. Well, there is no time like the present, I suppose. Bear in mind, though, that I shall probably be disinclined to oblige you, after the sneaking way in which you insinuated yourself into my carriage."

"No," said Neddy. "I must talk with you in *private*."

"Well, you shall just have to wait, then, won't you?"

"Who are those men, Aunt Bell?" asked Edwardina. "And why do they follow us wherever we go?"

"Those men, my poppets, are going to be your new fathers."

"Are they, really?"

"Yes, indeed, provided your mothers have the wisdom to be guided by me."

It was the kind of summer afternoon that begins beautifully, with three tender cumulus puffs in a clean, blue gentian sky, and which, inside of an hour, turns a solid dirty white, after the clouds have merged and knit themselves together into one continuous lint blanket. Hidden behind this vaporous veil, the sun beats through with all of summer's vigor and none of its benefit, so that the air turns oppressive and muggy and people sit about listlessly longing for naps. It was beastly inside the landau. Neddy and Eddie fidgeted uncomfortably.

"I advised you to stay at home, but you wouldn't hear of it," Arabella reminded them. "Now, you can put your heads out of the windows, if you like; there's a bit of a breeze to be got that way, but you're not to make a sound. If you behave to my satisfaction, I shall buy you each a fruit ice when we are finished."

The carriage arrived at last, and Arabella alighted from it, beckoning to the two officers.

"My young charges are hot, thirsty, and bored, as I suspect are you. If I send my coachman out to find refreshments for you all, would you consider sitting in the park for an hour and entertaining the children?"

They nodded gratefully, and Frank added, "God bless you, ma'am," under his breath.

Sir Corydon-Figge's library/office (for Arabella's meeting was at his house) was lit by three soaring, arched windows. The great man was seated at a polished wooden table, piled with books and papers, writing in a ledger that looked like Euphemia's. But Arabella reflected that it was a common commercial ledger, the sort that might be purchased from any stationer's.

Corydon-Figge stood up and bowed, with a somewhat distracted air. He was stern looking, solidly built, and Arabella surmised that he made a wonderful impression in peruke.

"I shall defend you when the time comes, Miss Beaumont," he said, "but I am afraid I shall not be able to do you much good. Circumstantial evidence is quite sufficient to hang a man—or a woman—under our present amateurish and practically non-existent police system. And, after all, you are a highly celebrated courtesan."

"What has that to do with it?" she asked, feeling herself on the defensive.

"I am not judging you," said the attorney. "I am merely giving you the benefit of my experience in these matters. Executions of women are always popular, and the execution of a rich, beautiful woman of a certain reputation is bound to be the sensation of the year. There are also certain . . . political considerations."

"Pray, sir, elucidate."

"The regent spends enormous amounts of money on himself, as I'm sure you're aware. Money which might otherwise be used for the public good. People are seething over this, and over the length of time it is taking to pass a reform bill, to say nothing of the Catholic question. The weather is hot just now, and everyone is irritable. Summer is riot season, you know, always a dangerous time. So, if the government gives the people a spectacle—the execution of a famous courtesan, for example—complete with fireworks and free gin . . ."

"Are they planning to do that?"

"I shouldn't be surprised if they were . . . it would certainly please the rabble. And a pleased rabble is, by and large, a peaceful one. I am sorry, my dear. I do realize that you are innocent. Glen*deen* has told me everything. But barring the apprehension of the real murderer, I am afraid that you will be selected as the one to pay the price for this crime. It *is* a deuced interesting one, isn't it? Several people have been to see me already about this business of the memoirs."

"I do not comprehend you, sir."

"Miss Ramsey's memoirs. You are supposedly featured in them, which is presumed to be the reason you killed her. All of London is looking forward to reading her book. It's expected out this winter."

The stunned look on Arabella's face told the story for her.

"How is it possible you have not heard of this? *A Clean Breast,* it's called. One of those tell-all scandalous things which names names and goes into salacious detail. I expect it will be doubly spectacular, now that the author has been martyred for it."

"Sir, I beg you will excuse me, I feel . . . rather . . ."

"Good lord, madam! You are as white as a sheet! Pray, put your head between your knees! I'll ring for brandy!"

Arabella was unaccustomed to placing her head between her *own* legs, and the novelty of this position soon had the effect of restoring her to herself, whereupon she was ushered back out to the carriage.

Memoirs! Of course! Why had she never thought of it before? People don't get murdered for private reflections in their private diaries! But the threat of *publishing* those private reflections . . .

"Good lord," she said aloud. "How could I have been so stupid?"

"What do you mean, Aunt Bell?" asked Eddie gravely. "You are the cleverest person in the whole world!"

Neddy clapped one hand over his mouth and pointed at his half sibling with the other: She had broken the silence edict; therefore her fruit ice was forfeit.

"No," said Arabella. "Eddie not only gets her ice; she gets *two,* for being such a darling. Now hush, both of you; Auntie needs to think."

But it was too close in the landau for that. Arabella had the top put down, to the children's joy—it wouldn't matter *now* if her frock was soiled. The world's cleverest woman put up her parasol, to ward off that unseen yet dangerous sun, whilst Eddie blew kisses out the back to Constable Dysart, who had seemingly managed to win her heart in a mere hour and a half.

The rest of the way home, Arabella stared straight ahead of her, like any properly bored aristocrat, as she thought about Sir Corydon-Figge's reply to her final question:

"Do you know who the publisher is?" she had asked him.

"Yes, that damned fellow who runs *The Tattle-Tale*—Oliver Wedge."

Chapter 11

Evening Festivities

A gaily wrapped package of a chapter, in which Constance nearly gets her head shot off, the flavor of human flesh is re-veal-ed, the vicar behaves foolishly, sex scandals are exposed, and a pair of bedtime stories is related. The evening concludes with a séance and a turtle.

As has been seen, the domestic staff at Lustings was a small one, for the house was not large, nor was Arabella fastidious. Hence, a lot of details (dusting, andiron polishing, rug beating) were ignored until they reached the state where something *had* to be done about them. Extra help was frequently brought in for parties, though. Belinda's birthday dinner, for example, required no fewer than six girls to assist Mrs. Molyneux, for the cook had outdone herself, as usual.

"I wouldn't be here, of course, except that I want the money for a new gown," sniffed one of the kitchen assistants as she sat, snapping green beans into a pot.

"Is that right?" asked her companion. "I was only too glad to get this job! We haven't et proper in a couple of weeks!"

"Well, I suppose I mustn't blame you then," said the other munificently. "People must eat, after all."

"But why ever *shouldn't* I want to work here? For the matter of that, why shouldn't *you?*"

"Well, I mean to say! Those Beaumont sisters are no better than they should be, are they?"

"Oh, yes, but you have to admire their style! You know you'd do what they do yourself if you had half the courage."

"What, me? Live a life of sin? Not likely, my girl, not likely! *They* may be lapping in the life of luxury now, but *I'll* go to heaven when I die."

"Hmph. That must be a great comfort to you."

"Here, look sharp, you two! And mind what you're doing!" cried Mrs. Janks. "You've mixed about the green beans with the strings you've just pulled off them!"

She rolled her eyes at the ceiling and muttered, "Nothing in all creation so empty-headed as a couple of girls!"

Up until now, little mention has been made of the male members of Arabella's staff—the grooms and gardeners who lived over the stable and carriage house. They don't really come into our story very much, but they were there, just the same, and for Belinda's birthday party they were all brought into the house and pressed into service as footmen, which assignment they quite enjoyed. For it not only gave them the excuse to wear livery (something they usually did only when driving one of the coaches) but also afforded the opportunity to flirt with the household servants. Not much of an opportunity, though, for Mrs. Janks was very much on top of things.

All this running about downstairs has quite tired your narrator. Let us therefore go up to the quiet haven of Arabella's bedroom, where we shall find the Beaumont sisters calmly trying on their evening wear and making last-minute adjustments thereto. They were not alone, for Constance had dropped in, ostensibly to see whether she might be of assistance with wardrobe selections, but actually, Arabella thought, she was probably only there to be irritating.

Whilst Arabella sat on her bed, chusing shoes from an impressive collection arranged upon the coverlet, Belinda tried on various jewelry combinations at the dressing table. Constance, like some gigantic non sequitur made flesh, amused herself by standing in front of the cheval glass and trying on Arabella's traveling cloaks and winter bonnets.

"You know, Arabella," said she, "I've been thinking."

"Oh, dear."

"Yes. You'll be up there, on the gallows, and the spectators will be down beneath you, won't they?"

"Constance . . ."

"A lot of the men will undoubtedly try to look up your dress, the filthy pigs!"

"Constance, if you wouldn't mind . . ."

"So why not cheat them? Cheat them, I say! Wear gentleman's breeches under your gown!"

"Constance, if you don't get out of here, I shall shoot you," said Arabella, taking the duke's pistol from the nightstand drawer and pointing it at her.

Constance paled. "You . . . you wouldn't . . . not *really!*"

"As they say, 'might as well hang for two murders, as one.' "

"They don't say that," said Constance. "Do they?"

"Oh, Constance," chided Belinda, who couldn't properly see what was happening. "Why must you always be so pessimistic? Bell finds you intensely irritating, and sometimes I do, too." She leaned in toward the looking glass, holding a pair of sapphire and diamond drops to her ears.

"I'm not a pessimist," Constance replied haughtily. "I'm a realist."

"O-ho! A realist, did you say?" asked Arabella. "Is that why you think Elliott Sheepleigh will come back to you? Is that why you affect the dress of someone a tenth your age? No, you are supremely annoying. I am going to count three, and then I am going to shoot you. One . . ."

"You wouldn't dare!"

"Two . . ."

"Belinda! Make her stop!"

"Three!"

Just then, Neddy put his face round the door.

"Aunt Bell, I must speak to you!" he wheedled.

"Not now, Neddy. As you can see, Miss Worthington has a prior claim upon my attention."

She sent a shot rattling past Constance's head and out the open window. Constance screamed.

"Help! Help! She's going to kill us all!"

"No—not everyone. Just you."

Constance scuttled out of the room like a polecat on two legs.

"I wish Puddles would give me lessons on this thing," said Arabella, peering down the barrel of the pistol. "I think I am supposed to clean it out now or something, and I haven't the faintest idea how one does that."

Neddy stood transfixed. "Oh!" he said at last. "The most wonderful things *do* happen at this house!"

"Go along now, Neddy," scolded Belinda. "Aunt Bell and I are trying to get dressed for dinner. You should be dressing, too."

Neddy left them reluctantly.

"Good-bye, Bell!" Constance called up from the garden. "See you at nine o'clock!!"

"Not unless you want to miss dinner!" Arabella called back. "The invitation said *eight* o'clock! Silly cow," she muttered. Then she sighed and replaced the pistol in the drawer. "Tell me why we're friends with Constance, again?"

"We grew up together . . . ," said Belinda, dabbing a bit of scent behind her ears.

"I hardly think *that* sufficient reason."

". . . and there aren't many women with whom we *can* be friends. Also, Constance has the most amazing connections when it comes to shopping."

"Oh, yes, you're quite right," said Arabella. "I had forgotten that."

* * *

In the brief interval that ensues before the official commencement of a dinner party, there inevitably comes an awkward lapse of a few moments to upward of half an hour between the arrival of the first guests and the household's being ready to receive them. On this occasion, Arabella found herself seated upon a sofa with John Kendrick, who had presented himself early, from sheer excitement. She was shewing him her album.

As we know, all young ladies keep these. They serve as repositories for the sort of small, useless trash one finds oneself powerless to throw away, and prove extremely useful in awkward moments like this one. Arabella was fortunate in having a great many artists as friends and contributors, which automatically made her album a *little* more interesting than most, and the fact that these selfsame artists had filled it with naughty caricatures of the Beaumont sisters rendered it absolutely priceless. There were some poems, too, and a few pressed flowers and things, but Kendrick didn't really mind what he looked at, so long as he was able to sit beside Arabella and be alone with her.

She turned the page to a ribald sketch by Thomas Rowlandson, featuring the prince regent and bearing the caption: "London Britches Falling Down!" It was decidedly improper, and Kendrick laughed heartily at it.

"You're such a puzzle, Mr. Kendrick," said Arabella. "One moment you appear to be shocked by impropriety, and at the next instant you laugh at it! I don't believe there could be another such churchman in all England."

"That is probably true," said he. "For if I could have chosen my profession freely, I should never have set my sights upon the church."

"What would you be then, if you could?"

"Oh, nothing! Like my brother! I should be rich and indolent, and spend all my time in amusing myself. Although I suppose I would spend *some* of it on worthy causes. Actually, I would spend a *lot* of time . . . and money, on worthy causes. Rather like I do now, in fact, only I shouldn't always have to bring God into everything."

"And do you bring God into everything now?"

"No, I don't. But I feel damned guilty whenever I leave Him out."

"I believe you do more good than you know, Mr. Kendrick, with or without invoking the Deity. But a great many poor people find solace in religion, you know; people who might otherwise give way to despair."

"Yes," said Kendrick. "The church's main advantage to the aristocracy is that it keeps the destitute humble, quiet, and out of the way. I feel such a hypocrite sometimes."

"I can understand that," said Arabella. "This century has got off to a dreadfully wicked start. Wouldn't it have been interesting to live back in the days of man's innocence?"

"When was that, precisely?"

"In the time of Lucretius, for example. The Romans strike me as having been particularly good at enjoying themselves."

"My dear Miss Beaumont! The Romans were *dreadful* bounders!"

"But how could that be? I am referring to the time preceding the birth of Christ, so they cannot be accused of un-Christian-like behavior. After all, you can't expect them to become Christians retroactively!"

"No, but . . . if you attended church once in a while, you would know this: The church teaches us that man was innocent, until he tasted the apple."

"That hardly seems fair."

"No, indeed!" cried the rector, with sudden passion. "It is *extremely* unfair, as a matter of fact! I have good reason to know that man was innocent until the church told him he *wasn't*."

Arabella closed her album. "I think the other guests have started to arrive. Let us go and greet them, shall we?"

The dinner party was a great success, largely owing to the hostess's inspired practice of engaging the entire table in a general discussion, rather than insisting that her guests limit their conversation to the persons seated to either side of them.

The dining room also played a part in the general conviviality, for its unusual color, a pale yellow, faintly tinged with green, looked very well by lamplight, like a warm patina on a bronze canary. A large and extremely opulent chandelier hung from the coffered ceiling, its swags and pendants of crystal drops reflecting the light from the oil lamps upon the dark-oak side table, a piece of furniture that was varnished and polished until it looked like milk chocolate. And the profusion of wine goblets gathered at each place promised that no one should have to wait for one glass to be refilled without refreshing himself from another.

They were twelve to dinner. In addition to the family, Mr. Kendrick, and Constance, Arabella had invited Thomas Rowlandson, hero of Ackerman's front window, and sporting something of a bay window himself, now that he'd reached his fifties; Leigh Hunt and Charles Lamb, two handsome young journalists; Richard Brinsley Sheridan, author of *School for Scandal*; and the Right Honorable John Ward, 1st Earl Dudley.

It had not been easy to find enough clever people for her table at the end of the season, but Arabella had managed: Rowlandson, Hunt, and Lamb, who all worked for the newspapers, had to stop in town late in order to earn their bread. Sheridan was on the point of leaving, and the earl was taking a holiday from his demanding mistress, who had gone on to Brighton ahead of him.

Naturally, everybody wanted to know how Arabella was getting on with her investigation. She told them about Euphemia's memoirs and was shocked to hear that most of her guests had known about them all along.

"Some of us were fair quaking in our boots to think what Miss Ramsey might decide to share with the world!" Leigh Hunt confessed. "Not anymore, though. Thank you, Miss Beaumont, for dispatching her when you did."

"I have not killed Miss Ramsey, Mr. Hunt."

"Haven't you?"

"No."

"Hmm. Well, whoever it was killed her must have been a blackmail victim."

"What is 'blackmail'?" asked Neddy.

"That is what it's called when you threaten to expose somebody's secret, or reveal something shameful or criminal about them, unless they agree to give you what you want," Mr. Sheridan explained. "Usually what you want is money, but occasionally it is goods or services."

"Oh," said Neddy. "So I blackmailed you yesterday, Aunt Bell, when I threatened to tell Miss Worthington you were leaving unless you let me come with you in the landau."

Fortunately, Constance, who was speaking to her server about the fish course, missed this remark, and on hearing the assembled company break into spontaneous laughter rightly assumed that she would not have understood the joke, even if it were explained to her.

"The murderer might have been anybody, really," said Mr. Lamb. "Many people had reasons for wanting her dead. I rather expect they will pin it on you, though, Miss Beaumont, because they've got your paper knife, and that is the only evidence they *do* have. If you haven't an airtight alibi, I wouldn't give a brass pin for your acquittal."

"That will do, Mr. Lamb!" cried Belinda, with a rare display of indignation. "This is my birthday party, not the Spanish Inquisition!"

"Quite right, Bunny," said Arabella. "I officially declare the subject closed!"

"Oh, wait, though," said Constance. "Did you ever find the sailor?"

"Yes, and no," Arabella replied. "We had no sooner established his identity than we learnt he'd sailed for Borneo, where he will almost certainly be eaten by savages before he can come back to testify. And that is all anyone is going to say on this topic."

"Are we allowed to discourse on *related* topics?" asked Rowlandson, smiling.

"That depends. What were you thinking of saying?"

"Only this: If all of us were marooned on a desert island, whom would you eat first?"

"Oh, I should start with Miss Belinda," said Mr. Hunt, who was seated next to her. "So plump and succulent, like a little duckling!"

The first course being brought in at that moment, the company shouted with mutual delight at the dish on offer: a platter of roast ducklings.

"Have you ever tasted human flesh, Selwyn?" asked the earl as he tucked into his bird.

"Matter of fact, I have. In Africa, you know."

"I suppose you're going to tell us that it tastes like chicken?"

"Not a bit. More like veal."

"Do you think our bodies really taste like veal, Mr. Hunt?" Belinda whispered, blushing a little.

"Only the calves," he replied with a smile, reaching under her gown and squeezing the back of her leg.

As her guests passed into the drawing room and the supper dishes were cleared away, Arabella went out onto the terrace. Mr. Lamb's cheerful allusions to her certain doom had depressed her spirits, and she felt she would like to have a few moments alone. But this was not to be.

"Miss Beaumont, are you feeling quite well?"

"Quite well, Mr. Kendrick."

The rector came over to stand next to her, resting his elbow on the balustrade.

"I want you to know that were it not for my spiritual obligations, I should have called Lamb out for being so tactless."

"Called him out? Wouldn't that have been going a bit far?"

"Well, perhaps," he admitted, with a self-deprecating smile. "But surely, you don't have any real cause for worry? Even if you don't solve the crime, I can't imagine they could hold you accountable for it. You're famous throughout the land!"

"Yes, which is precisely *why* they would like to hang me. Wonderful publicity, you know. There always is, when they execute a woman or a celebrity, and I happen to be both. Think of the opportunities for instructive sermons! For selling newspapers! For hawking souvenir gallows during the public spectacle! Don't worry, Mr. K.," she added, seeing his expression. "I *do* expect to solve it, you know."

"I hope you will permit me to continue to offer my services."

"You anticipate me, sir. I was just thinking that perhaps you should reconsider your position. After all . . . you could jeopardize your career!"

"I do not think so. For offering to help the generous patroness who paid for our new chancery roof?"

"You exaggerate, Mr. Kendrick! I merely *helped* to pay for the Effing roof!"

She leaned against the balustrade and smiled at the stars. "No friend of those Effing Sunday school children could fail to do as much."

Arabella looked enchanting out here, in her diamond tiara and black-and-silver-striped gown, with her shoulders gleaming white in the moonlight, above the little tassel that hung from each capped, puffed sleeve. She was so noble in her suffering, so greathearted, and so solitary.

"Miss Beaumont," said Kendrick. "Perhaps this is not the ideal moment in which to say this, but I . . . that is, if you . . . if you think you could be happy as my—"

"Mr. Kendrick! Arabella! What are you doing there?" shrieked Constance, coming through the French doors. "It's time to cut the cake!"

Meanwhile, on the other side of the wall that defined the Lustings demesne, a handful of men began to unload the contents of their wagons. They worked silently and in the dark, lest a noise or a light betray their presence to those within, with scarves tightly wrapt round their mouths and noses.

Inside the house, though, a spirit of openness and good cheer prevailed, and the birthday confection was a work of art—all over pink icing, with Belinda's name spelled out in pale-green sugar.

"My sister Fanny had a cake last week," said Eddie, "with six candles!"

Whereupon Constance, who was more than a little tipsy, felt she should object. Getting up from the table, she tiptoed unsteadily to her hostess's chair and bent down to whisper in her ear. But in any event, Constance was not discreet. The entire company heard her:

"I hope I am as open-minded as the next person, my dear, but isn't Fanny rather young to be having sex scandals?"

"*Six candles*, Constance," said Arabella. "Now pray, sit down, so that Bunny may open her presents."

Constance was wearing a white bandage draped across the top of her head, "to be prepared," as she put it, in case Arabella should try to shoot her again. She was also wearing a black pelisse over a white gown and bright orange lip rouge, so that she looked like an enormous gentoo penguin. This, her hostess reflected, was a slight improvement over the infant-in-swaddling-clothes look and the scuttling-polecat look effected by Constance's scramble from the bedroom, but the woman's idiocy was beginning to get on her nerves.

The usual custom of providing brandy and cigars for the men, who remained in the dining room whilst the women removed themselves to some parlor to drink tea, was not observed on this occasion, for Arabella had no intention of spending an hour sequestered with Constance. As far as the hostess was concerned, the more persons on hand to prevent Miss Worthington from jumping naked into the shrubbery, or to dissuade her from (intentionally) dressing up like a rabbit, the better. So everybody retired to the drawing room, though Hunt, Lamb, Dudley, and Sheridan (Hunt the Lamb, Dudley Sheridan!) lingered in the passage with Rowlandson, to examine Arabella's collection of his rarer prints. These were ranged along the rich green walls in ornate gilt frames and pertained exclusively to The Great Subject. Arabella felt no compunctions about setting them out where everyone could enjoy them, and her guests were appreciative of this attitude. Because, as Rowlandson explained, most of the people who purchased copies of these particular prints were gentlemen who kept them locked away in a drawer and only took them out when alone.

Eventually, all the guests found their way to the drawing room and settled on the floor there with cushions, cake, and glasses of port, whilst Mr. Sheridan presented a phantasmagoria, or magic lantern show (which could have been dirty, but wasn't), for the general entertainment.

Afterward, as the children were being led off to bed, the company was so comfortable on the floor in the dark that they lingered there, and Constance suggested they hold a séance for Euphemia's spirit, using the Indian Ojah mat which Sir Geoffrey had given Belinda.

"Excuse me, ma'am," said Fielding, curtsying, for shew, before company. "Miss Eddie is calling for her story."

"I must ask you all to wait till I've come down again," said the hostess, and she went up to Eddie's room, where she sat in the chair next to the child's bed and took her little hand. Their fingers interlaced.

"You're going to hear this sooner or later, dear," said Arabella, gravely, "and I'd just as soon you heard it from me first."

"Are you going to tell me the facts of life, Aunt Bell?"

Her aunt regarded the child with surprise.

"Good heavens! Don't you know those already?"

"Yes, I do, as a matter of fact."

"I should think so, too, considering the family that you come from! No, I was going to tell you 'The Parable of the Curious Hen.' It's not a pretty story, but it has the merit of being a highly instructive one."

"Is it a real story, or have you made it up yourself?"

"Yes. There was once a hen, who yearned to see the wide world, or at least, the bit of it that existed beyond her own farmyard. She used to complain and cluck about it all the time, and her friend the duck was jolly sick of listening to her.

" 'You should be happy with what you have,' said the duck. 'For there is nothing but danger and treachery Out There.'

"But the hen disregarded the duck's good advice, and one day she ran away into the woods.

" 'Here it is,' she muttered, for the hen was always talking to herself, 'the wide world! Hmpf! Can't say as I think much of it—it's dark in here, and the bugs taste nasty.'

" 'Do they?' asked a weasel, who was passing by. 'I don't eat bugs, myself, but I think *my* food is exceptionally tasty.'

" 'Is that so?' asked the hen. She had never met a weasel before and didn't know the first thing about their feeding habits. 'Well, I'm nothing if not adventurous, sir! Perhaps we could have dinner together sometime!'

" 'Now that is what I call a capital idea,' said the weasel. 'Come along, and I'll introduce you to my mother.'

"But when they arrived at the weasel's burrow, his mother saw her stupid son in the company of a plump chicken, which he hadn't bothered to kill, or truss, or anything, and she lunged out with bared teeth, worried lest their dinner should escape. The hen, who could fly a little, flew up into a tree, and sat looking down on the weasels, panting.

" 'Now, why did you do that, Mater?' asked the weasel, angrily. 'Couldn't you see that the hen was coming to us of her own accord?'

" 'You know nothing about it!' snapped his mother. 'Hens must be tied up! They bolt at the slightest provocation!'

" 'That one believed herself to be our guest.'

" 'Ha! No chicken in the world could be so stupid!'

" 'She was, though. Congratulations, madam; you have just deprived us of a splendid, risk-free roast chicken dinner!'

"The hen, hearing all this, learnt a great deal from it, and sent up a prayer to the god of the fowls: 'I have been a stupid chicken, indeed!' she sobbed. 'But if You will let me leave this forest alive, I promise to go straight home and never talk about leaving again!'

"She waited until the weasels had gone and then flew down to try to find her way home. But it was late by then, and chickens' homing instincts, never strong to begin with, aren't worth a tinker's damn in the dark. The hen was soon caught and eaten by a fox."

"Is that the end of the story?" asked Eddie.

"That is the end of the hen's story," her aunt replied, "but you haven't yet heard what happened to her friend, the duck. The second part of this tale is about her, and it is called 'The Duck Who Stayed Behind.'

"Soon after the hen disappeared, a new servant was assigned to the fowl yard. This woman was a lazy slattern, and the poor, neglected duck spent days, and sometimes weeks, pent up in the duck house without seeing daylight. Eventually she developed foot rot and softening of the bill, which latter affliction made it nearly impossible to eat—on the rare occasions when there *was* any food, that is. And you may imagine the stench in there!

" 'Well,' thought the duck, 'although this isn't what I would call a pleasant existence, at least I am safe from the wicked world in here.'

"But there she was wrong. As a result of all the suffering and privation which she had undergone, the duck stopped laying. And one day the servant hauled her out by the neck, plucked her naked whilst she was still alive, which hurts like anything, and then chopped her head off. Now go to sleep, darling."

Arabella's stories usually sprang from her own immediate circumstances, and on her way downstairs she pondered the origins of the tale she had just told. Primarily, she was feeling intense resentment toward the unjust turn things had taken. Arabella had started out disadvantaged by bad parents, had been plunged into poverty, had found an alternative to starving, and finally had pulled herself and her family into a very agreeable, if socially unacceptable, mode of living, all through her own efforts. Now it seemed she was to be destroyed at last, and through no fault of her own. Like the chicken in the story, she had taken a chance and braved the dangers, only to be broadsided by the unforeseen. If she had chosen the duck's path, however, she would have been plucked and roasted long before this. Life was unfair. To women, anyway.

She returned to the drawing room in a thoughtful mood. Her guests had unrolled the fortune-telling mat in her absence and set out the odd-looking pointer. Mr. Hunt and Belinda, with their fingertips touching upon this, were waiting for something to happen.

At Arabella's entrance, Mr. Kendrick rose from the floor.

"Good night, Miss Beaumont," he whispered, "and thank you for a wonderful evening."

"Are you really going, Mr. Kendrick?" Arabella whispered back.

"I think I had better," he replied. "Witchcraft games, you know. As a churchman there are certain activities with which I may not risk being associated."

She felt disappointed. Not, of course, because anything could possibly have happened between herself and the rector there on the floor—Mr. K. was a staunch, if reluctant, man of God, after all—but she found his presence . . . comfortably reassuring, and the prospect of his absence made her sad.

He kissed her hand and, there in the darkness, pressed it to his heart, whilst everyone else was watching Mr. Hunt and Belinda operate the pointer.

"It . . . it's *moving*," Belinda whispered, in awe. "Are you moving it, Mr. Hunt?"

"No," he replied nervously. "I thought *you* were!"

A hush had fallen over the company. Everyone strained forward to see the name that was being spelled out by forces from beyond the veil: "I . . . AM . . . EUPHE . . ." And suddenly the shadows seemed to deepen; the candles grew less bright. Darkness was closing in. All eyes were focused on the Ojah mat, now, and the only sound to be heard in the room was the concentrated breathing of the guests.

"MY . . . MURDERER'S . . . NAM—"

The earsplitting scream was so loud, so unexpected, that two of the guests actually fell over. As Constance drew in her breath to shriek again, Arabella precipitously clapped a hand over her mouth, and Mr. Rowlandson grabbed a candle, thrusting it toward the spot on the carpet that was riveting Miss Worthington's attention.

Neddy's turtle, Stupid Looking, stood with his front paws planted in Constance's cake and his mouth full of icing, blinking his little red eyes in the candlelight.

Never had any creature in Arabella's experience so fully deserved its name.

Chapter *12*

COOLNESS UNDER FIRE

*In which Belinda relates how she met the princess,
Fisto irritates his listeners, The Tattle-Tale office
is vandalized, and Arabella keeps her head
whilst engaging the enemy.*

Arabella slept late the next day, and so did the rest of the household, apparently, for by the time she had groped her way to the breakfast table she found her uncle and Mrs. Janks seated there—he in a dressing gown, she in morning *dishabille*—serenely spooning up soft-boiled eggs and smiling at one another over their newspapers.

"I love the way you live, my dear," said Sir Geoffrey, looking up from *The Morning Post* as she came in. "It's all so natural and easy! A taste of simple rusticity in the heart of London! Where else would I be able to enjoy a morning's tête-à-tête with Mrs. Janks, and not be censured for it, eh?"

Belinda staggered in, dropped to her seat, and clasped her head in her hands.

"Ooh," she groaned. "I've got *such* a head!"

"Ooh," groaned Fisto in his cage. "I've got such a head!"

"Shut your beak!"

"Shut your beak! Shut your beak!"

Arabella rose and flung a cloth over his cage. "Now I see why you named him Mephistopheles, Uncle!"

"Quite," said Sir Geoffrey, swallowing his tea. "That bird

has a most uncanny sense of timing. Well, am I to have the pleasure of your company today, Arabella, or shall I go to my club?"

"I am interviewing a witness this afternoon, Uncle."

"Oh, well, then; Belinda?"

"I am supposed to be dining at Montagu House, although," said Belinda, grimacing, "I'm not sure I am feeling up to sauerbraten and bloodwurst today."

"However *did* you manage to become such a favorite of the Princess of Wales, my dear?" asked Mrs. Janks. "Things have been so hectic round here lately that I never had a chance to ask you."

"Oh, it's a silly story, really."

"That doesn't put me off, lovey; I'm keen to hear it."

Belinda made a brief show of searching back through her memory and reluctantly preparing herself to tell a tale, but actually, she was enormously pleased; at Lustings, it was usually Arabella who told the stories. No one else ever got the chance.

"Well, let me see . . . I first encountered Caroline of Brunswick, Princess of Wales, at Hyde Park, in the Serpentine."

"*Near* the Serpentine, d'you mean?" asked Sir Geoffrey.

"No. *In* it."

He looked confused for a moment. Then his face cleared.

"Ah! The two of you were in boats. Is that it?"

"No. I was strolling along the walk near the lake when I heard someone sobbing in the direction of the water. At first I came over all gooseflesh, as one *would,* thinking, you know, of the unhappy ghosts of drowned people—children fallen in, and maidens forced to marry men they despised, that sort of thing. But on reflection, I surmised that a ghost would most likely produce a ghostly sort of sound, and this was quite a robust style of weeping. More like a bellow. So I parted the reeds and peered cautiously through them, where I beheld Her Royal Highness, in a not-very-tasteful but obviously expensive gown, long gloves, tiara, the lot, standing in water up to her knees and wailing like the world was ending. It was apparent from where I stood that she was quite drunk. So I coughed deferentially and asked whether she required assistance, whereupon she cried,

" '*Oh!* I think I have killed a *swan!*'

" 'Surely not,' I replied. 'Swans are singularly hearty fowl. But what has happened, exactly?'

"She turned her face toward me, all streaming with tears, and said, 'I tried to ride one, and it *sank!*' "

Everybody laughed, even Arabella, who'd heard the story before. A moment after they stopped, Fisto laughed, too, beneath his calico drapery, sounding like a roomful of people.

"How does he *do* that?" asked Belinda wonderingly.

"Better you should ask *why*," said Arabella.

"Then what happened?" asked the housekeeper.

"Well, I coaxed the princess out of the water and wrapped her in my shawl, and eventually we found her attendants. She kept insisting that I had saved her life, and I was made to go home with her and stop the night there. The princess finally allowed me to send a messenger to let Bell know where I was, but by the time he arrived, my poor sister was half-distracted with worry, and on the point of calling out the militia."

"Which I could have done, too, given my connections," said Arabella. "Bunny has been practically living over there ever since. Is there any breakfast today, Mrs. Janks? I'm half-starved!"

Just then, the door opened behind her, and Arabella heard Fielding's cheerful voice:

"Here we are, madam! Shirred eggs and bacon, currant scones and raspberry jam, grilled kippers and coffee!"

"Oh!" cried Arabella. "That's capital! How did you know that I was so hu—"

But turning round, she beheld an astonished Fielding, carrying a tray with nothing on it but tea and toast.

Under his covering, Fisto laughed, again.

"Bell," said Belinda, "I believe we should move Fisto to the aviatory after all."

"Yes. Perhaps you're—"

Just then, Mrs. Janks began to choke violently upon her toast. Sir Geoffrey was at her side in a moment, thumping her on the back, whilst Belinda and Arabella poured out a tumbler of water. Gradually, the coughing subsided, and the poor woman lay back against her chair in a state of semi-exhaustion.

"There, Mrs. Janks!" said Arabella with relief. "You gave us quite a fright!"

The housekeeper sat up again, clearly agitated and gulping air like a fish, so that she might speak at once.

"The newspaper . . . !" she croaked. "There, in the news-paper!" She jabbed at an article with her finger.

But Arabella looked first at the masthead.

"Oh, no," she groaned. For Mrs. Janks had been reading *The Tattle-Tale.* "I can't," said Arabella, handing it to Belinda. "Read it out for us, Bunny."

"Duke Shields Murderous Mistress from Justice!

"Just what does the Duke of G think he's about? That he has used his considerable politi-cal influence to keep a dangerous criminal out of gaol is hardly in the public's best interest! That he will sail for Portugal at the end of the month probably is, as we are bound to be better off without him, but what of *her?* A wanton strum-pet, who, despite every material advantage, sold the family carriage and threw away a life of re-spectability in order to hire herself out at so much an hour to all comers! (Or not, according to her customers' personal tastes and abilities!)

"The informed reader knows that A has had no children. What? With as many opportunities as she has had? She *has* borne children. She must have done! Has not A's own sister been seen on the grounds of their walled estate, at all hours and in all weathers, digging holes with a garden spade? What is she burying, you ask? Boxes, large enough to contain infants, all decorated in swags and flowers; the very acme of funerary art! If they were her own newborn babes, the girl would be far too weak to dig. Make no mistake about it: She is burying A's children! No doubt she is being forced to!

"Duke or no duke, shall this monster go free? Shall she be allowed to wander our streets, murdering babies at random for the rest of the month? Or shall she be arrested NOW, before she has the chance to murder again?"

Sir Geoffrey was speechless for a moment, but Belinda wasn't.

"How does he know about my boxes? Have you discussed them with him, Arabella?"

"Of course not. Why should I want to tell him a thing like that?"

"How else could he know?"

"He probably bribed the gardener."

"Oh. But why does he persist in writing lies about *you?*"

"Do you mean to say that you actually *know* this brute?" her uncle asked fiercely.

"*Know* him!" cried Belinda. "Why, Arabella positively . . ."

But she caught her sister's expression just then, and her voice died away in her throat.

"We met him at the creditors' auction," said Arabella,

"where he represented himself to us as a sympathetic supporter of my cause. Apparently, such was not the case."

"I won't stand for it!" cried her uncle. "Where's my horse-whip, by gad?"

"Now, now," said Mrs. Janks. "None of that, Sir Geoffrey." She turned to Arabella, who was opening her letters. "This here Miss Wiggle-Diggle, or whatever she calls herself, that you're going to see today. Is she the last of your interviews?"

"Yes. Well, no. Sort of. I am also intending to speak to the prince regent at the grand fete. Not to actually question him, you know, but to get myself introduced. And I shall attempt to make him like me."

"Now surely, you don't suspect that *he* murdered Euphemia?"

"He might have done," said Belinda. "Remember last year? When his brother murdered his own valet?"

"You don't say!" exclaimed Sir Geoffrey. "Which brother?"

"Cumberland. It was in all the papers here. I wonder you never heard about it, Uncle Selwyn. Don't they have newspapers in Kandy?"

"I never read 'em. Too busy in those days. Now that I've retired it seems I have some catching up to do. What happened?"

"Cumberland woke the household in the middle of the night, screaming that he'd been attacked. They found him with his sword drawn, and bleeding from both hands. In the next room, his valet was found in bed, with his throat cut so deeply he was practically decapitated. A bloody razor was discovered on the other side of the room, so obviously it wasn't a suicide, but that's precisely what the jury decided it was. They said the valet had attacked the duke, and then immediately killed himself, from remorse."

"Poppycock! Why should he have done that?"

"No one ever gave a reason. But some say there was a very *plausible* reason for the duke's having murdered his valet: Cumberland had raped the man's daughter, and the poor girl committed suicide when she found herself with child. Her father probably threatened to take the story to the newspapers."

"Damme! And the blackguard got away with it, you say?"

"Clean away with it," said Mrs. Janks. "Nobody never liked him to begin with, but mobs try to lynch him now, whenever he goes out."

"So you see," said Belinda. "That sort of behavior runs in the royal family. If Cumberland may kill a valet, why shouldn't the regent kill a courtesan?"

"Two courtesans," said Arabella, setting down her letters. "You see why I must go carefully here; this matter has to be handled with the utmost discretion."

"Oh," said Mrs. Janks. "I don't think he would, really. He's not a good prince, heaven knows, but somehow I don't see him going out and killing women in cold blood."

"Not him, personally; he would have paid someone else to do it," said Arabella. "The way he paid someone to steal my paper knife. If he has done this, I am a dead woman. If not . . . well, perhaps, if I befriend him, he will be moved to take pity on my situation. It seems to be my only hope now, as I have been unable to discover the murderer on my own."

"There is still time," said Belinda.

"Yes, a little. So, the prince regent is a suspect. Lady Ribbonhat is a suspect, too, but she has refused, absolutely, to meet with me, in her home or anywhere else. In fact, I have just received a letter from her." Arabella extracted a letter from its envelope and unfolded it. " 'Lord Sidmouth be damned!' " she read aloud. " 'Let him come and arrest me! Let him *try*.' "

"Well!" exclaimed Mrs. Janks. "Of all the . . . that woman is positively *common!*"

"I didn't really expect her to comply," Arabella admitted. "But writing to her felt so satisfying! It gave me an excuse to inform her that her departed husband was one of Euphemia's clients, and that Euphemia had written the word 'DIS-EASED' under his name."

"Oh, well done!" said Belinda approvingly.

"Of course, later I realized that she had actually meant to write 'deceased.' Euphemia was not an accomplished speller. Still, I need not explain that to Lady Ribbonhat."

Arabella put down her napkin, rose from the table, and kissed Sir Geoffrey on the top of his head.

"I am very sorry to leave you, Uncle, but after tomorrow I shall be at your disposal, up until the moment that the government disposes of *me*."

"I pray you, do not talk in that vein!" said Sir Geoffrey. "And don't worry about me—I shall spend the day at my club."

"You off to see Miss Jiggles, then, my dear?"

"No, Mrs. Janks, there has been a change of plan. I am going to Fleet Street, to confront that odious Mr. Wedge!"

Arabella dressed herself in a salmon-pink and lavender ensemble, which, on its own, made her look too vulnerable, so she added dark-brown chicken skin gloves. As she donned a pair of flat brown shoes to match, she thought fleetingly—wistfully—of the pretty little high heels so in vogue a generation ago, and how much more enticing her mother's feet had looked in those than her own appeared in these.

This time, as her carriage passed through the gate, a different sort of stench raped her nostrils.

"Trotter!" she choked. "Is that *shit?*"

"Yes, ma'am!" he replied, and gagged. "The human variety! Several cartloads, looks like! It's piled all around your wall, here!"

"Good lord! Well, don't stop now, Trotter, or I shall be

late for my engagement. Have the gardeners dispose of this when we get back, please."

"Right you are, madam!" he said, and grinned. "Long's I don't have to do it!"

Arabella had not written to say she was coming. Military tacticians maintain that surprise is often the most effective weapon of all, and such was the fact in this case, although the surprise was just as much upon her own side as her adversary's. For when she arrived, Arabella discovered *The Tattle-Tale* office in a state of complete chaos: chairs and printing presses overturned, documents all over the floor, a window broken. Oliver Wedge straightened from a crouch as she came in, both hands full of newsprint paper.

"You did this," he said accusingly.

"Indeed not," she said, removing her gloves and bonnet. "I have only just arrived, as you see."

"I didn't mean you, personally. You hired someone to vandalize my office."

"And why should I want to do that?"

"In revenge for . . ."

"Yes? Revenge for what?"

"For those . . . articles."

"Oh, come, Mr. Wedge. You can do better than that! You're a journalist! Words are your business! To which articles do you refer?"

"You *did* hire someone!"

"I did not. But I am beginning to wish that I had. Because whoever did this wasn't half-destructive enough! The people I should have hired would have done such a thorough job that you would never have been able to put this office back to rights! I merely came here today to confront you about 'those articles,' as you so euphemistically call them. Those vicious, biased, hate-mongering articles . . . I trusted you, Mr.

Wedge, with my life's story, and you twisted it into a degrading, personal condemnation."

Arabella had begun to straighten the room as she talked, not to be helpful but because she needed to be doing something to keep her hands from scratching his eyes out. Wedge had been retrieving objects from under the furniture, but he stopped now, to watch her.

"Not only have you gone out of your way to stir up popular sentiment against me," she said. "You have been withholding vital information!"

"My God. You're magnificent when you're angry."

"You're a liar," she cried, almost beside herself. "An evil, sneaking, selfish liar! How could you stand there? In that dead woman's apartment? Watching me hunt for clews, knowing that my life depends on finding out everything I possibly can, and simply 'forget' to mention that you're planning to publish her memoirs?"

"I'm not."

"I know that you *are*, Mr. Wedge. Half of London knows, evidently."

"That half is misinformed. I admit that I entered into negotiations with Miss Ramsey before she died, but I never actually *saw* the memoirs. And the manuscript was not amongst her personal effects. In fact, it has completely disappeared."

The room was very close, despite the open windows, and Wedge poured out a glass of water. From a handsome, silver-plated pitcher. Which had miraculously escaped being upset by the vandals. Or perhaps Wedge had brought it down with him. Arabella knew that he lived above the office. She accepted the tumbler. It was Waterford crystal. Wedge poured out a second one for himself.

"It is fortunate that these lovely things escaped destruction," said Arabella.

"They were upstairs," he said. "I brought them down just before your arrival."

"Did you? And why bring two of them? You did not know I was coming."

He took her empty glass, set it down, and moved in closer, but Arabella turned away from him to straighten the portrait, which was pronouncedly askew this time. She looked at it briefly, considering.

"Might I venture to ask you a question, Miss Beaumont?" Wedge's thrilling voice had grown deeper, softer, unmistakably intimate. He was looking at her in a particular way and standing almost upon her toes. Arabella checked the impulse to step back and then found that she really didn't *want* to.

"Is this . . . for publication?" she asked, turning to face him. Her own voice had acquired a husky timbre, owing to her sudden inability to breathe normally.

"No, no. In fact . . . I wrote those articles specifically to get you to come out here. Now that they've done their job, I won't need to write any more of them."

In the heat of the office, a curl had come loose. Wedge brushed it from her cheek and twined it round his finger. Then he removed her pins, one by one, until the famous auburn hair came tumbling down and fell about her shoulders in russet waves.

"Why not?" she asked. It required a great effort of will to control her diaphragm, which wanted to squeeze up against her lungs and force the air from them in short, sharp gasps.

"Because," he said. "After today, you won't need to find an excuse to come here. Nor shall I need to find one to come to you."

"What . . . was your question, Mr. Wedge?" she asked.

"Euphemia . . . Miss Ramsey . . . told me that she was intending to give you a section all to yourself, in her memoirs. And I wondered if you knew why that was?"

He pulled her close and planted a reckless kiss in the hollow of her clavicle.

"Yes. I think I may . . . enlighten you there. You see, Mr.

Wedge, in my capacity . . . as a courtesan to great and powerful men, I am the keeper of secrets which . . . could bring this nation . . . to her knees."

"Really?" he murmured. "To her knees? In front of another nation, who was standing up and unfastening his trousers?"

"My point is—"

"But surely, Miss Beaumont, *I* am the one with the point. And it's making no end of a nuisance of itself right now. . . ." He began to unbutton his breeches.

"Wait!" she cried. "Before this goes any further, I have to know something: Did you pay Euphemia any money?"

"Yes. I gave her one hundred pounds."

"But I thought you said you never saw the memoirs."

"I didn't. I gave her that money for . . . quite another purpose."

Oh, this was intolerable! She was angry and excited and jealous! Arabella was jealous!

"Why?" she demanded hotly. "Because you slept with her?"

Now it was Wedge's turn to be angry. "No, confound it! I *didn't* sleep with her! What do you take me for, madam? She was my mother!"

Chapter 13

READER, I F****D HIM

In which Arabella enjoys an afternoon's diversion and visits an artist's studio, more is learnt of Wedge and his mother, Lady Ribbonhat takes the initiative, and Miss van Diggle tells a lie.

"I only learnt who she was after my father died, when I discovered certain documentation amongst his papers," said Wedge. "Euphemia confirmed it herself. She had watched me grow up, from a distance, of course. But she never tried to contact me. Perhaps my father told her not to. I had always believed myself to be the child of his wife, you see. Do you suspect me of murdering her? But why should I? I had been hoping to make a tidy sum from her memoirs, and now that's all gone to dust. Kill my own mother? Me? A devout Catholic? We have rules about that sort of thing, you know. Besides, what possible grudge could I have against you? You beautiful, clever, fascinating woman! I'd never even *met* you, more's the pity. Think of all the time we have wasted! Let us waste no more, I implore you!"

Arabella cleared her throat. "May I see this documentation, please?"

"Why? Don't you trust me?"

"Mr. Wedge, I do not *know* you. I should be foolish indeed if I trusted you on so brief an acquaintance."

"Fair enough."

He vanished through a doorway and returned a few moments later, with a letter in his hand. "This contains a duplicate of the entry in the birth registry of the Church of St. Mary the Virgin, Little Ilford. And, yes, I went out there and saw the original myself. You are welcome to go and see it, too."

"Thank you," said she.

"You are welcome. Do you know, sometimes I wonder whether Euphemia ever wrote that book at all? It's a kind of 'emperor's new memoirs,' isn't it—all this hullabaloo and fanfare, with nothing to show for it."

"I have a kind of ledger of hers," said Arabella, observing him carefully, "with what look to be preliminary notes. Most of the pages have been torn out, though."

He shrugged. "It doesn't sound like enough for a book."

"It isn't. Mr. Wedge, do you know or have you an idea about whose names she might have listed on those missing pages, or why they were removed?"

"I don't. Perhaps the murderer does."

"I can understand why he might want to remove his own pages, but not why he should have torn out so many."

"Saving his friends, too, no doubt. Or perhaps he felt, if he only tore out his own reference, it might be possible for others to guess his identity through the process of elimination. You know, Euphemia told me some of the people she intended to include. I've forgotten most of them, now, but it wasn't only men. As I've said, you were going to have a section all to yourself."

Arabella decided not to tell him about the pages she had destroyed.

"Can you recall anyone else, Mr. Wedge? Specifically, anyone who might have known me, as well as Euphemia?"

"Yes, I can, as a matter of fact. Julia van Diggle, your duke's fiancée. Now are you satisfied?" he asked, clasping her by the arms and letting his eyes roam up and down her face.

"Not yet," she whispered. "But I'm sure that I *shall* be, provided that you are able, sir, to rise to the occasion."

"I already have," said Wedge.

And he showed her.

"I have never felt this way about anybody before, Bunny," said Arabella. "It was like . . . like being on fire, and praying that nobody would ever come along and douse the flames. I cannot get him out of my mind. The way he walks, the sound of his voice, his smell . . . and I keep revisiting the things that he said, over and over, without even consciously trying to. I don't suppose you know what I mean."

They were lying on Arabella's bed, for when she spoke intimately of Mr. Wedge, Arabella hadn't the strength to sit up.

Belinda snorted. "Certainly I know! I go through this *every time!* Does Mr. Widget feel the same way about you?"

"Mr. *Wedge* has not actually shared his feelings with me, but I suppose he must do, because it's rather like alchemy, is it not?"

"How do you mean?"

"Base metals. They attract . . . I think. Do you understand what I mean?"

"I understand the 'base' part," muttered Belinda.

"Well, *I* don't. I don't understand anything about the laws of attraction! When a man feels what he feels, what does he feel? Is it for you alone? Is it *because* you are you, or simply because you are *there*? I mean, are you the only woman in the world for him, at that moment, or would anybody else do just as well, and you just happen to be the most convenient?"

"I think it really depends upon the situation," said Belinda diplomatically. "Was he considerate? Did he make an effort to create a romantic atmosphere? Did you go upstairs to his bedroom, or did he take you to a nice hotel?"

"No," said Arabella faintly, into her pillow. "It happened in his office. On the desk."

Her sister said nothing for a few moments. "What a mess you must have left," she managed, finally.

"What do you mean?"

"All those papers, and the broken window and everything. I don't suppose either of you stayed to clean it up afterward."

"Oh, *that* mess! Well, no, you're quite right there."

"Bell. He didn't even have the decency to offer you a *bed*."

"He was probably too carried away to think," said Arabella.

"Yes. That was probably it."

"You disapprove, don't you? You think there was something 'wrong' about it."

"Not if he paid you."

"I didn't charge him. It wasn't a business transaction."

"In that case, yes, I do think it was wrong."

"I believe you to be right, Bunny." Arabella suddenly found that she *could* sit up. "And there was something wrong about the office, too."

"Go on."

"It had been vandalized, like I told you. It was a mess. But it was a *careful* mess. Nothing was actually destroyed. No ink was spilled. Presses were overturned, but there was nothing that couldn't be set to rights again in short order."

"That *is* strange. There was a window broken, you said."

"Yes, but from the *inside*. There was very little glass shard lying about, as most of it was out in the street. It was a small pane, too, not one of those floor-to-ceiling windows, which would have cost the earth to replace. The papers on the floor weren't scattered about so much as *fanned*, as if for easy retrieval."

"Interesting. Do you think Wanker did it himself?"

"I don't know what to think. And there was one other thing; the office was empty of people. Mr. Wedge was there alone. Aren't newspaper offices generally very busy places?"

"Arabella, I don't want you to see that man again."

"Why not?"

"Because he's dangerous. You feel it yourself."

"Yes, perhaps I do. But it doesn't make me want to stop seeing him, Bunny. It makes me want to see him *more*."

The next morning, Arabella visited the duke's fiancée, having rescheduled her interview from the day before. It was a tiring ride, and like Miss van Diggle herself, the way was gravelly, tedious, and devoid of interesting viewpoints.

On arrival, Arabella was shown into a fussy and over-heated parlor. Yet her reception was as cold as even Lady Ribbonhat could have wished.

"Why ask me?" sneered Julia. "I have good reason to want to see *you* swing, but why should I want to kill this Rowsey or Ramswell or whatever her name was?"

"Perhaps," said Arabella quietly, "because your name was listed in her book."

Julia blanched, and her hauteur vanished on the instant. "*My* name? But that can't be! There wasn't time!"

"Wasn't there?" Arabella decided to pretend, for the moment, that she understood this remark.

"I'd only just got back before she was killed."

"Yes? Why don't you tell me about that?"

"I've been in France for the last two months, and quite unreachable. Her letter was sent to me here, and it sat on the desk all that time with the other post, awaiting my return."

"Whose letter?"

"This Rowley woman's, of course."

"What did it say?"

"The same thing they all said; it was the same letter she sent to everybody, offering to let us buy ourselves out of her memoirs."

Arabella began to breathe rapidly.

"Do you still have that letter, Miss van Diggle?"

"No, of course not! I burnt the disgusting thing!"

"How much was she asking?"

"Three hundred pounds! Can you believe the impudence?"

"Scarcely. What else do you remember?"

"That she promised to tear out all pertinent sections upon receipt of my checque."

So! thought Arabella. Euphemia had torn out those pages *herself!* Therefore, the ones that remained represented only the people who had refused to pay!

"Miss van Diggle," Arabella said. "What damaging information was Euphemia threatening to expose about you?"

"That is none of your business. It has nothing to do with this matter."

"I think you had better let me be the judge of that."

"I absolutely refuse to discuss it, you impertinent baggage!" Julia sprang from the couch and rang for the footman. "I should be obliged if you would remove yourself from my house at once!"

"Very well," said Arabella, arising from her chair in a movement that somehow managed to express self-possession and resignation both. "In that case, Miss van Diggle, I have just five words to say to you: 'French ambassador,' and 'White House, Soho.' I should be able to turn up quite a lot of information about you on my own, since you were foolish enough to use your real name."

The footman appeared in response to his summons.

"Get out!" snarled Julia. "I don't want you!"

After he had left the room, Arabella gathered up her things.

". . . And, lest you try to claim later that I haven't played fair with you," said she, "I shall tell you now exactly what I intend to do with the details as soon as I've got them: I shall turn them over to *The Tattle-Tale* editor. Can you imagine? What a grand edition he'll have! My public execution and your private career!"

"No, wait!" cried Julia. "What will happen if . . . if I tell you myself?"

"Then I shall take your revelations to my grave, whenever I get there. I give you my word on that."

"How do I know I can trust you?"

"You don't. But if you force me to hunt down the story myself, I pledge myself equally to expose you. You believe that, don't you?"

"Yes."

"Well. I'm not the sort of person who would give my word on one thing, and mean it, and give it on another matter and forget to. You will just have to accept that, for it's the best I can do."

"Please, Miss Beaumont," said Miss van Diggle, her manner completely changed, "I pray you will sit down. May I offer you some refreshment?"

"Thank you," said Arabella. "I should appreciate a cup of tea."

Tea was duly brought, and poured, and handed to her with perfect cordiality.

Miss van Diggle took a cup for herself, too, as though they were old friends.

"When I was younger," she said, "I used sometimes to work weekends at the White House. It was fun, you know; my girlfriends and I did it for a lark, and to make some extra pocket money. Papa was very mingy, and he never let me have any."

Here she began to cry. Arabella offered her handkerchief, but Miss van Diggle had her own.

"One day, Mr. Hopper, the proprietor, offered me something special. He said there would be a lot of money in it for me, if I would consent to a three-way, but that the customers were very well-known, and I had to promise never to say anything about our activities. It was Euphemia, of course— she was already getting old, by that time—and the French ambassador, who was younger, and wanting some variety. So I started spending my Saturday afternoons at the White House, mostly in the gold room, but sometimes in the silver, with the two of them."

"I see. And have you continued to see the ambassador, on your own?"

"No! That was years ago! It's all finished now, I swear it!"

"Miss van Diggle, you have been in France for the past two months, I think you said? What were you doing there?"

Julia flushed a dull red.

"Well, well," said Arabella quietly. "Still playing in the muck? When you're engaged to the duke? In some circles, that would not be considered very nice."

"I suppose you'll tell Glen*deen,*" said Julia sulkily, her eyes on the carpet.

"Do you? When I've already said that I won't? Perhaps promising never to tell a thing conveys no meaning to your mind, Miss van Diggle, but it does to mine, I assure you. Who else have you told about your weekend romps with Euphemia and the ambassador?"

"No one! I swear it!"

"But," said Arabella lightly, "you also swore that you'd stopped *seeing* the ambassador. Swearing things to me, now that I've seen what that means to you, carries no weight whatsoever, Miss van Diggle. But I shall not tell the duke. I shan't need to: Once your engagement is announced, there will be plenty of people wanting to profit from what they know—your former clients, fellow prostitutes . . . if you're silly, you'll be buying their silence for the rest of your life."

"And if I'm sensible?"

"You'll break it off with the duke and marry a nobody."

On her way home, Arabella rapped on the carriage window with her ruby ring. "Greek Street, Trotter. Thomas Lawrence's studio, if you please."

She found the artist at his easel, putting the finishing touches to a portrait of Sally Siddons, who was not present, having died some eight years previously. His left hand held a long stick, tipped with a soft ball of cotton wool wrapped in chamois leather. This was pressed against the canvas, so that his right hand, resting on it, remained absolutely still whilst he added the eyelashes.

"Arabella!" cried the artist. "You've come to sit for me at last! Come on, then; off with your clothes!"

"Not now, Thomas; I'm here on business."

"Wonderful! Strip for me, darling!"

"Not business of that kind." She studied the portrait on his easel. "Still painting Miss Siddons?"

"Always. Forever. I am as true to her memory as I was to the woman herself and won't you *please* remove your clothing, Arabella?"

"Later, perhaps; just now I am in rather a hurry—I need to ask you about a portrait you painted of Oliver Wedge. Do you remember it?"

"I should think so—I only finished it ten days ago! It's hanging in the editor's office at *The Tattle-Tale,* if you want to see it."

"I know. I have just lately come from there, and could not help noticing that, though it's an uncommonly wonderful portrait, as all your paintings are, it does not actually look like the subject. Which isn't your style, Tom; your portraits are very like, as a rule."

Lawrence had returned to his work and was now painstakingly adding the light to Sally's eyeballs.

"Hmm. Well, it looked like him at the time. I only paint what I see, except when I need to improve on reality. I cannot be answerable for sitters who go and change their appearance afterward."

Arabella thought about this on the way home, but her thoughts were interrupted when, as the coach waited at the corner for a herd of cattle, no less a personage than Lady Ribbonhat herself came up to the window.

"You have lost him!" she exulted, and for a moment Arabella didn't know whom she meant. "Now that my Henry is free of you, he shall marry a woman of high standing! A woman beyond reproach!"

"Ha!" Arabella replied. "The only difference between Miss van Diggle and myself is that I am open about who I am, and she is not. Also, I cannot be absolutely certain about this, but I think she may have had even more lovers than I."

Whereupon Lady Ribbonhat smacked her stick smartly against the wheel of Arabella's coach and took herself off.

Chapter 14

HIS ROYAL HIGHNESS, THE FAT GIT

*In which Fisto earns his keep and the regent holds
his right and left fetes, proposes a name change
for Arabella, and discusses a cunning peace plan.
General conversation embraces the Sphinx's nose
and the originality of Mrs. Cornelys.*

"Mrs. Janks, would you send the gardener's boy in to
me, please?"

"Gardener's boy. Into me please. Gardener's boy," Fisto
repeated.

Arabella had recently had his cage moved into the library.
She had shut herself in there, too, for several hours. Now she
sat at one of the tables and reviewed her investigation notebook whilst Belinda reclined on the window seat, writing in
her diary.

"What do you want with the gardener's boy, Bell?"

"It's an idea I had from Casanova."

"But, Bell! The lad's not fourteen!"

"Exactly. Boys that age have twice the stamina of adult
males. Now don't speak for a moment, Bunny; I'm trying to
concentrate."

Arabella started to go over the contents of her notebook
once again. Every time she added some new piece of information to it, she had to read the collection as a whole, and
not in any particular order, for in this way she sometimes

gained startling new insights. Thus, flipping back and forth between pages, she read:

Things Found Out

A sailor, Jack Furrow, paid (by a gentleman) to steal my knife.
ER was going to publish her memoirs
ER was Wedge's mother
ER was blackmailing her victims

Helpful Persons & Their Uses

Belinda—anything I ask
Mr. Kendrick—ditto
Mr. Wedge—(?)
The Duke—custodian, found me a lawyer
Sir Corydon-Figge—criminal defense
2 Bow Street Runners—misc. errands

Clews

a ledger remnant
a death threat letter (probably Lady Ribbonhat's)
dead horse, dead sheep
cartloads of human shit

Persons to Talk To

my staff
Euphemia's landlady
Euphemia's neighbors
Euphemia's blackmail victims
(ER had no family, friends, or recent lovers.)

Scene of the crime: ER's room
Condition of location: already messed about and emptied when
   I got there
Look for: documents, letters, notebooks, diaries

Suspects

The Duke of Glendeen (via his mama)
Motive for killing ER: keeping his father out of the memoirs.
Motive for framing me: making his mother and fiancée happy.
Whereabouts at the time: with me.
Attended my party? Yes.
Behavior: distant, lately.
Other factors: got me a reprieve (could be guilt). Hired a
   lawyer.

Julia van Diggle
Motive for killing ER: memoirs would have spoilt her chance to
   marry DG.
Motive for framing me: jealousy.
Whereabouts at the time: abroad.
Attended my party? No.
Behavior during interview: Haughty, at first. Then frightened.
   Then compliant.
Other factors: I have dirt on Julia.

Charles Edward Beaumont
Motive for killing ER: unknown at this time.
Motive for framing me: annuity.
Whereabouts at the time: one never knows with Charles.
Attended my party? No, & wouldn't have paid anyone to steal
   my knife, either.
Behavior: haven't seen him in weeks.
Other factors: Not like Chas. to murder someone in order to

frame me in order to get money. His mind doesn't work that way.

Oliver Wedge

Motive for killing ER: None. Had every reason to want her alive.
Motive for framing me: great copy.
Whereabouts at the time: unknown.
Attended my party? No.
Behavior: inconsistent.
Other factors: Break-in seemed staged. Portrait doesn't look like him.

Lady Ribbonhat

Motive for killing ER: keeping her late husband out of the memoirs.
Motive for framing me: thinks she'll get the house.
Whereabouts at the time: unknown.
Attended my party? No.
Behavior during interview: Refused interview. Generally hostile.
Other factors: Enemy of long standing. Shall have to request magistrate's direct involvement. Leave this for now.

Arabella looked up when she heard a knock at the open door.

"Hello, Moses," she said, addressing the handsome, half-Gypsy lad. "Did you enjoy dressing up for my party the other night?"

"Yes, miss."

"Would you fancy dressing up again? Like a rajah, this time, and earning nearly as much as a rajah does?"

"Why, yes, miss!"

"Good. Here is the costume. You may go put it on in the kitchen, and then come and show me how you look."

The boy returned in a violet turban, a gold-embroidered vest, scarlet Turkish trousers, and crimson shoes with curly toes.

"Yes," said Arabella with satisfaction. "You look splendid, Moses!"

Belinda was staring at her, goggle-eyed. "I must protest this, Bell! You yourself have said—and I agree with you— that children and animals are off-limits in this house!"

"I made that remark in reference to business, Belinda," said her sister, unhooking Fisto's cage from its stand. "This is a personal matter. Now listen, Moses: You're to take Fisto here down to the Royal Exchange, and stand in a central spot, where everyone is certain to see you, holding this sign."

Belinda got up to look at it:

TALKING MYNAH FOR SALE £50.

"Trotter will take you down in the barouche with a food hamper to see to your wants, and he will bring you and Fisto back again at six o'clock this evening. I shall pay you a crown a day to do this for as long as I wish you to."

"A crown a day . . . ! And in the *barouche?* Crikey! But you'll never sell him for fifty pounds, miss! No, nor even twenty-five!"

"I realize that. I do not actually wish to sell him. Now, here is the bird. Whenever he falls silent, urge him to speak by quietly saying the words 'Lady Honoria Ribbonhat . . .' "

Thus prompted, Fisto launched into the verse Arabella had taught him:

> "Lady Honoria Ribbonhat
> Has bags and bags of gold,
> But what is the possible use of that?
> She's so dreadfully ugly and old!"

"I want the bird to say his piece as much as possible throughout the day," Arabella explained. "You're to see that he does, no matter how tiring it may be to listen to him. Will you do that?"

She had to shout this last part, in order to be heard over Belinda's laughter.

"Yes, miss!" cried the boy, grinning from ear to ear. "For a crown a day I can listen to him for the rest of my life!"

"Well, you need not go so far as that. I'm guessing no more than a week at the outside. And I shall change the verses from time to time, Moses, so that you . . . and the public . . . do not get too bored."

On the nineteenth of June, the Prince of Wales held a grand fete at Carlton House, in celebration of his ascension to the regency. He had never been a popular prince, nor, from the looks of things, would he be a popular regent, but his parties were popular—the *haute ton* had been talking of this one for weeks. Everywhere an atmosphere of excited expectation reigned, despite grumbling in some quarters about the financial strain on faltering government resources. There were also those who deplored the want of proper filial feeling. After all, George was only regent because his father had gone mad, hardly an occasion to celebrate. Nevertheless, the regent's critics planned on attending, too. Everybody was coming who had been invited, for it was only a matter of time until poor, mad King George died and the regent would be crowned, prompting yet *another* large and expensive party.

"Do you know the difference between the king and the regent?" one buck asked another as they ascended the steps of Carlton House.

"I could tell you the difference, yes," replied his companion, with a smile. "But I've a feeling that your explanation will prove more entertaining than mine."

"Well, then, the king throws fits, and the regent throws fetes!"

A lady, overhearing this remark, struck the wag with her fan, and his friend laughed. But that laugh, uttered on the very threshold of the festivities, was the last one heard all evening. For the party, despite—or perhaps because of—its elaborate presentation, was a complete failure. There were several reasons for this, but the author will perhaps be pardoned if, instead of listing them, she escorts her readers thence and permits them to draw their own conclusions.

First, you will note the size of the throng. Around three thousand persons are gathered here, although, probably, the dining table being a mere two hundred feet long, not all of them will be entertained to supper. The enormous conservatory has been made up as a bower and planted with shrubs, flowers, small trees, and patches of grass in order to simulate the out-of-doors. The aforementioned table, set in the midst of all this, extends beyond the confines of the room—across the palace's entire length, in fact—and at one end a silver fountain pours an endless stream of water into the moss-lined channel comprising the centerpiece. Come closer and observe the lotuses and other aquatic plants, floating on the surface. Pretty, aren't they? And look—there, just underneath the lily pads—do you see the silver and gold fishes, swimming from one end of the endless table to the other? What do you suppose all this has cost?

The prince regent sits proudly at the head of this table, just back of the fountain, surrounded by his particular friends and personally waited upon by seven servants. Of course, many more servants attend to the guests, not one of whom has seven, or even one servant all to himself.

A man inside a suit of fourteenth-century armor walks

jerkily about, attempting to bow at random and generally be-
having like an idiot. Behind the regent, and indeed, all about
the room, tables displaying pitchers, goblets, vases, urns, trays,
and other decorations of gilt and sterling have been set up
wherever there is space for them. The items serve no practical
purpose in being here but are exhibited just for shew. Above
the scene is a gigantic replica of a royal crown, with the initials "GR" all illuminated. You might be tempted to laugh at
the pretentious absurdity—I know I am—but, as has been
stated earlier, the suffocating pretentiousness of the setting
prevents it.

The other mirth-suppressing element must be the guests
themselves: foreign ambassadors, London's principal nobility
and gentry, government ministers, distinguished military and
naval officers, prominent aldermen and magistrates, and even
a number of church officials, who should have known better.
The tone set by these worthies and their ladies is one of stiff-
necked self-consciousness, with everyone intent upon pre-
serving the illusion of flawless protocol, regardless of its effect
on the human spirit. How could anyone, being present, laugh?
And how could anyone, telling about it afterward in reassur-
ingly familiar surroundings, fail to?

At precisely 1:00 am, the party was over and the high and
mighty were abruptly shown the door.

"What industrious servants you have, sir!" sneered a de-
parting guest, who'd had a half-finished plate of raspberry
trifle practically snatched from her hands. "So remarkably
quick to clear away the supper dishes!"

"Yes. They're very efficient," said the regent. "I expect
they'd like to get to bed." He yawned ostentatiously. "I know
I would!"

Thus "Prinny" hurried the ladies out, not minding if he
were rude, because he was practically king now and could
behave as he liked. But a careful observer might have noticed

that some of the lords lagged behind, studiously trying to look as if they, too, were on the point of leaving when, in fact, they weren't.

After the last grand gown had swept from the room, the servants began dashing about in earnest. Prinny consulted his watch and showed it to his butler.

"Fifty-nine minutes, Enderby! I want everything cleared away and set up again exactly as it was at eight thirty this evening!"

Then he left to change his clothes.

A few moments after his re-entry, Lady Hertford was announced, whereupon a portly woman of middle age ascended the dais to curtsy before him.

"No, Izzy, darling!" cried the regent, raising her himself. "It is I who should kneel to you!" He kissed her hands with fervor and then, smiling lecherously, whispered something in her ear.

"Still," Lady Hertford complained, "I am insulted that you have asked me to your second party, Prinny, rather than your first one!"

"Yes, I might have done," he said, "but I was certain that you would have a much better time at this one. I know *I* shall!" He tucked her hand beneath his arm and began to stroll with her about the room. "Some people find holding two parties on the same night excessive, but I do not think it is. Brummel assures me that I am just as entitled to two fetes as I am to two hands. Haw! Deucedly clever fellow, Brummel."

The other guests had begun to arrive, for the regent had wished to celebrate his ascendancy with the people he wanted to have, as well as with those whom he'd been obliged to invite, but as far as the ladies were concerned, he could scarcely have mixed the two groups. Besides, this arrangement gave him an excuse to wear *two* gorgeous outfits, rather than just the one. The regent loved to dress up. He loved to gratify every whim, in fact, and the spending of large sums of money was as necessary to his well-being as air itself.

"When I was younger," he had once observed to the Earl of Yarmouth, "I used to deny myself very little in the way of indulgences. Then I graduated to denying myself nothing whatever. But now that I've matured, I regret the folly of my undisciplined youth. These days I deny myself everything but the best."

Nobody liked him, really. He was greedy, unkind, and morbidly self-absorbed. But Prinny could always count on full attendance at his balls and parties, offering, as he did, the best food and spirits. Arabella couldn't begrudge him his tastes. They were not quite *au fait* with her own, perhaps, but they at least reflected an appreciation for the exceptional, and had resulted in a number of strange-looking public works which would be left as a legacy to the nation. Arabella had only been invited to the "left fete" but was keen to go, for she had never met the sovereign-in-waiting and was looking forward to lording this fact over Lady Ribbonhat, who hadn't met him, either.

"Naturally, La Ribbonhat is acquainted with the mad *king*," Arabella chattered to Belinda as Doyle affixed ostrich plumes to her coiffure.

"Naturally," Belinda echoed, attempting to be supportive.

"But, well, I *mean* . . . that's the old king, isn't it?" Arabella asked, fastening the clasps on her blue topaz bracelets. "And after tonight, when I shall be able to say that *I've* met the *new* one, Lady Ribbonhat will be absolutely devoured by envy. She wasn't invited at all, you know, because of her late husband's allegiance to . . ." Her voice died as she caught sight of her sister's sad face in the mirror. "Oh, Bunny, dearest! I *am* a pig! Can you ever forgive me?"

Belinda had not been invited, either. For the regent so loathed his wife, Caroline, that no crony of hers was allowed within spitting distance of his royal person.

"Of course, Bell; after all, I'm not the one who's about to go to gaol. And you know, this might actually save you—if you make a favorable impression on the regent, he might decide to grant you a royal pardon."

"That is precisely what I am thinking." Arabella stood up and turned around for her sister—a vision in pale-orange satin. "How do I look?"

"Like an apricot tart," said Belinda approvingly.

"Good enough to eat?"

"Yes, amongst other things."

It may seem strange to the reader that Arabella would pause in her efforts to save her own life just to attend a party, but bear in mind that she had long desired an invitation to Carlton House. This would not be an official acknowledgment, of course; the occasion was a gathering of sinister persons and she was herself a woman of ill repute, but it was as close as Arabella would ever come to an official presentation, and she was not about to let a little thing like a murder interfere with one of the most important moments of her career.

Carlton House, the regent's official residence, was a horrifying hodgepodge of architectural styles, something like a cross between a Roman villa and the Society for the Prevention of Cruelty to Horses. Behind its massive columns and ridiculously gigantic pediments, the structure meandered off in all directions, as though portions of it were seeking a means of escape from the rest of it.

Arabella was met on the steps by Scrope Davies, one of her particular friends, and escorted by that worthy gentleman through an immense hexastyle portico with Corinthian columns, through a scarlet foyer, to a two-story entrance hall ringed with Doric columns of yellow marble. She shuddered with unexpected nausea at the clashing colors and hideous immensity of it all, for Carlton House was truly a monument to bad taste. They passed through an octagonal room and various ugly spaces, until at last they reached the Great Conservatory.

"Oh, I say!" exclaimed Davies. "What a truly princely show! My eyes are fairly dazzled by this surfeit of glamour! How do you find it, Miss Beaumont?"

"Well, it is truly, as you have indicated, too much to take in all at once. It is also not original, being a copy of the Rural Masquerade given at Carlisle House in 1776."

Arabella knew she was waxing pedantic, but others had begun to gather round her and she could never resist the temptation to show off.

"The redoubtable Mrs. Cornelys had the idea first and, to my mind, realized her vision much better. *She* didn't find it necessary to display her silver and gilt plate—one never sees those things in a forest glade, after all. And her guests did not sit at a formal dining table, but upon the 'ground,' where they ate picnic-style, out of hampers on the 'grass.' "

"Now, how would you know that?" asked Lord Allen. "You could scarcely have been out of swaddling clothes in 1776."

Having stabbed her interlocutor with an icy glare, Arabella now proceeded to slash and cut him with it:

"As a matter of fact, Lord Allen, that was some years before I was *born*. No doubt, because you yourself have adopted the use of wigs, corsets, and makeup in an effort to preserve the appearance of youth, you assume that everyone else has, also. But if you were not too proud to wear your spectacles, you would see that I do not affect youth's outward shew, because I possess it naturally. As I was saying, Mrs. Cornelys did not go in for elaborate dishes. The hampers contained simple foods: asparagus, strawberries, crayfish, and hot roast chickens. Simple, yes, but elegant. How do I know this, you ask? I read about it, in Casanova's memoirs. Apparently the regent did, too."

"Well, perhaps it is not possible to be truly original in the matter of grand celebrations, with so many centuries of royal pomp having preceded this one," said Lord Worcester. "Nevertheless, you must concede that His Highness is an innovator architecturally; look at the Brighton Pavilion."

"The Brighton Pavilion is modeled on Sezincote," said Arabella, "and I am on that account disobliged to entertain your assessment of His Highness's originality."

At that point, she was claimed by the dashing Lord Alvanley, to the evident relief of her listeners and consternation of all the men who had hoped to partner her first. Alvanley, who had also been present at the earlier party, took advantage of the intervals when they actually danced side by side or faced each other with hands clasped high over the heads of other couples to entertain Arabella with gossip about the "great ladies" he had observed there earlier in the evening.

The regent didn't dance very much, preferring to stand on the sidelines with a crony or two and look on while his guests galloped past him. During one of their turns about the room, Arabella overheard the Earl of Yarmouth, a famous roué and the son of Prinny's current mistress, murmur her name.

"A damned fine woman, Yarmouth!" the regent replied. "Too young, though."

The prince regent had always preferred his women fat, old, and relatively unattractive. Now that he, too, was all three of those things, for he had always been two of them, his tastes seemed more appropriate. But that was no comfort to Arabella, who had hoped to charm him.

After the first set had finished, Alvanley brought his partner forward.

"Your Highness. May I present Miss Arabella Beaumont?"

She curtsied, well aware that the regent was looking down her décolletage.

"But there are so many Arabellas these days!" he protested. "It seems every second or third woman I meet is an Arabella! It dates you, my dear, such a common name. And from what I hear, you're quite an *un*common woman."

She wasn't sure how to respond to this. "What would you have me called then, Your Majesty?"

"Oh, I don't know. Something timeless and wild, perhaps, smelling of the out-of-doors and hillsides. Something entirely rare and original, like . . . 'Heather.' "

" 'Heather'? But do you really think that name suits *me,* sir?"

"How should I know? I've only just met you. It's sure to suit somebody. I'll have to think about it." He wandered away, whereupon another gentleman immediately appeared to whisk her back to the dance floor.

After another hour or so of rigorous exercise, Arabella was ready to sit down for a while in order to catch her breath and fan herself a little, for the conservatory was most infernally hot. Its glass walls ran with the condensed exhalations of the assemblage, putting her in mind of her own perspiration, which she could feel tickling its way down her back and between her breasts. Everywhere she looked, Arabella saw men and women with red faces and streaked makeup, and the knot of admiring gentlemen which stood close about her did nothing to help keep the temperature down, but Arabella did not really mind, for men were her métier, after all. She was on the point of accepting a glass of warm punch from her latest partner when she glanced to her left and noticed the regent headed purposefully in her direction. And Arabella's admirers, seeing him too, melted away like the ice that had cooled the punch bowl some hours ago.

His Royal Highness took the chair next her own. He was all affability this time, and Arabella felt reassured. I won't say a word about my case, she thought. That should impress him with my forbearance and good sense.

Instead, they spoke of the war.

"I could end the whole thing in twenty minutes, you know," said the regent, "but Parliament won't let me."

"How should you proceed, Your Majesty?"

"I'd simply ask Napoleon up to the palace."

"Of course!" said Arabella, nodding. "How sensible! Then the two of you could discuss matters over dinner, and come to a mutually sustainable agreement!"

"No—I meant I'd have Napoleon up to the palace, and shoot him. Think of all the artworks I could save, all the priceless things they're butchering over there. Have you heard about the Sphinx's nose? Shot off, by gad! Shot off, by Napoleon's soldiers!"

"I *own* the nose, Your Majesty. One day, if I live long enough, I shall go to Egypt and glue it back on."

Naturally, Arabella didn't really own the nose, which, before a cannonball smashed it to pieces, probably weighed half again as much as she did. But in her art collection there actually was a nose from an ancient statue of roughly the same color as the Sphinx, and she reasoned that this was close enough, should she ever be asked to produce it.

"What do you think of my little party?" asked the regent presently.

"It is . . . entirely characteristic of its begetter, Your Majesty," she replied.

"And how would you describe my costume?"

"If a foreigner to these shores were suddenly to come into the room, having no prior knowledge of England, he should nevertheless be able to guess who, out of all this company, was its prince."

"Should he, madam? Why? Because of the richness of my attire, or because, where he hails from, the ruler is inevitably a 'fat git'?"

Arabella stared at him, dumbstruck, whilst a blush of deeper hue suffused her previously light-pink countenance.

The regent stood up. "If you'll excuse me," said he, with a curt bow, "I must go now, and . . . how did you put it? 'Get stuffed.' "

He turned and left her abruptly, and as she sat there, trying to collect herself, a man whom she did not know took the chair lately vacated by His Majesty.

"Cut you, did he?" asked her sympathizer. "Well, you know, that's just his way—the regent never forgets a slight. It's too bad, really: He will soon be the most powerful man in the world. As George IV, he will be in a position to create a truly enlightened society if he wants to, leading his nation to-ward a glorious new renaissance. But I very much doubt that will happen," said the man, shaking his head. "Because, as you have just seen for yourself, he has one of the most repul-sive personalities ever to shame a royal house."

Arabella, who was fanning herself vigorously in an effort to extinguish her blush, remained silent.

"Personally, I have no patience with people like that, even though it is my job to," the fellow continued. "The entire royal family, with the possible exceptions of the mad king and Princess Charlotte, have devious, criminal minds."

As the newly appointed Danish ambassador to Britain, this man should not have been saying such things at all, much less to a total stranger, but he was a kind person and hearing the regent cut Arabella had outraged his sense of de-cency. He had only just arrived in the country and as yet had no idea who Arabella was.

"Do you know," he said, "that someone recently tried to blackmail him? Can you even imagine such a thing? Black-mailing the sovereign? Yes, but that isn't the worst of it. I'm told that the regent had this person killed, and then arranged to blame his crime on a completely innocent person. In my country, royalty does not behave in this way." He nodded to himself. "In fact, I like my own country so much better than this one that I think I should go home, and find a profession that allows me to stay there." He drained his cup, stood up, and offered his hand to Arabella. "May I have this dance?"

She went through the motions automatically, without being mentally present for any of it. She was doomed. All her hard work had come to nothing in the end. She would never be able to prove her innocence now. And then she overheard the regent on the sidelines, discussing herself once again.

"See her, Brummel? The one dancing with the Danish ambassador? That's the radiant little murderess we've been hearing so much about! Ha! She won't be looking quite so radiant when she's dancing at the end of a rope, though, will she?"

Chapter 15

HOBJECTS LOST AN' FOUND

*In which the solution is found in a box of oddments,
Neddy goes too far, and Arabella puts it all together.*

The rising sun discovered an exhausted Arabella, sitting despondently on the end of her bed and removing her dancing slippers. It was quite clear to her now that "Prinny" had arranged Euphemia's murder after she threatened to expose him. It was also clear that he fully intended to let Arabella hang for it.

Once again, her thoughts turned toward death. Was there an afterlife? Mr. Kendrick thought so; Lucretius did not. According to her favorite poet, death was the absolute cessation of existence. And yet Lucretius had committed suicide. Arabella shuddered to think of him—of anyone—submitting voluntarily to permanent oblivion. She was much more comfortable with his views on *existence:* "Avoid pain. Pursue pleasure and beauty." Well, she had done that, hadn't she? My life has not been a long one, she reflected, but most of it has been perfectly splendid.

A straying sunbeam had lit a fire in the deepest recesses of her red glass elephant, whose humped back and head protruded from the box on the floor. She lifted it out. This is one of the things that has *made* my life so splendid, she thought, turning it in her hands and admiring it from all sides. It really was a most exquisitely wrought piece. She placed it on her nightstand, where it would always be the last thing she saw before blowing out her candle.

Once the elephant was removed, the remainder of the box's contents were revealed—what the auctioneer had called lost an' found hobjects—and with half her mind absorbed in her own melancholy affairs, Arabella began to sort through these. A pocket watch, a ring . . . She was struck by something and went to the boudoir to check her notebook, taking the box with her. Yes, Euphemia had listed these items in her ledger. Apparently, she had placed them in this box herself, owing to their universal adherence to a particular concept. Apparently, they were assurances left on account by cash-poor clients:

> **silvr wach—for hand jobb (dozent wurk)—fred**
> **hanker cheefe—fr one garder—henry**
> **gold plate—fraudd venturs—alley**
> **spektakels—cosmo forgott these**
> **smuddy ring—sam—in paymint for fyndinge him a redhed**
> **minachre portrat of charlie—for cash lone**

The watch was tarnished and, as Euphemia had noted, didn't work. But any fool could see that it was silver. Evidently, the creditors had given this box a lot number without inspecting the contents!

Next was the gentleman's handkerchief, which Euphemia had evidently exchanged with its owner for one of her garters. Love tokens? There was a *G* on the handkerchief. And the family crest of the Dukes of Glen*deen*. Interesting. Euphemia had once held Puddles in thrall. Or this might just as easily have belonged to his father. Poor man. It was not surprising that he should have preferred Euphemia's company to that of Lady Ribbonhat.

Next, Arabella examined the denture: an upper plate, shaped like a palate, to which four porcelain front teeth were

attached. This was coated with some sort of carbon residue—
soot, most likely—which came off on her fingertips. But
when she put the plate down to wipe her hands, a yellow
gleam showed through where her fingers had been. Gold!
The creditors had been careless indeed! She wiped away the
rest of the soot and had a closer look. Eighteen-karat gold
and stamped with a goldsmith's mark. The teeth had been
very realistically done, but for some reason, the artist had left
a gap between the front two. She checked the ledger, again:
"gold plate—fraudd venturs—alley." "Gold plate" made sense,
now. It was a *dental* plate, not a dinner plate, but "fraudd venturs"? In an alley? What was that supposed to mean?

Obviously, the "spektakels" were of no value, except to
their owner. These had not been left on account, according to
the ledger, but simply forgotten by one of Euphemia's clients.

The next item was that intaglio ring. Purple glass, showing
an amorous couple engaged in the dog position. Hold on . . .
one of them *was* a dog. Interesting. And finally, the miniature
portrait of a handsome young Regency buck. The thing was
exquisitely executed but mounted in a rough wooden frame
that wasn't even gilded. Well, thought Arabella. I shall give
this to Eddie, so that the child will at least have *something* of
her father's. For it was a portrait of Charles.

The entries all made sense to Arabella now, except for the
denture, which, owing to the gold, was clearly the most valuable thing in the collection. Arabella decided to follow up on
it, and wrote forthwith to the vicar of Effing:

> *Dear Mr. Kendrick,*
> *Would you be so good as to check this for me?*

[Here she painstakingly copied the mark on the dental
plate.]

> *Find out, if you can, the goldsmith's identity,*
> *and, if you find him, ask whether he recalls the*

name of the person to whom he sold a gold dental
plate with front-gapped porcelain teeth.

With many thanks,
Arabella Beaumont

Just as she was finishing, there was a knock.

"May I come in, Aunt Bell?"

Neddy's sharp, wicked little face appeared around the door. "I must talk to you. It's terribly important."

"Important to whom, Neddy, to you or to me?"

"Well, to *me,* of course," he replied. "But if you don't hear me out now, I shall just keep dogging you until you give in. You know what I'm like."

Arabella sighed. She did know. "Very well. What is it?"

The child let go his hold of the door and swaggered over to her like a little bantam rooster. He walks just like his father, she thought. He was still in his nightshirt, and Arabella realized, with a start, how early it was.

"I heard Mother telling Sarah-Jane that you refused to lend her five thousand pounds to start up her business. She said you were a tightfisted hussy. I told Mama I was going to tell you what she said unless she gave me a puppy. But she wouldn't. So I have. That's the way blackmail works, isn't it?"

"Yes, Neddy," said Arabella. "That is exactly how it works. But the decision to reveal incriminating information should always be very carefully considered. For instance, if it is going to hurt *you,* as well as your victim, you may wish to review your position. In this case, it was ill-bred and extremely stupid to come and tell me this. Why have you done so? And how could you do such a hateful thing, to Polly, of all people?"

Neddy gave a contemptuous snort. "I'm not going to let her off, just because she's my *mother!*"

Sometimes, a casual phrase, uttered by a person uncon-
nected with one's own problems, can illuminate the darkness
and reveal the truth to us in a blinding flash.

But first things must come first.

"Fair enough, then," she said. "Do you enjoy these visits
to Lustings?"

Neddy shrugged. "Better here than at home, I reckon.
Food's better."

"Well, I don't suppose it will matter that much to you
then, but now that you have created bad blood between your
mother and me, you shan't be coming here anymore."

Perhaps Arabella's words had as strong an effect upon
Neddy as his own had produced upon her a moment before,
for the boy suddenly burst into tears, whereupon his aunt,
beyond words irritated by his selfishness, stupidity, and
wretched, peevish wailing, promptly banished him from her
presence.

Once the quiet atmosphere of her boudoir was restored,
Arabella considered Neddy's illuminating remark: "I'm not
going to let her off, just because she's my *mother!*" If this
comment were attributed not to Neddy but to Oliver Wedge,
it changed everything. For Arabella, with little experience of
the criminal world, had taken it for granted that sons did not
murder their mothers. Especially not good Catholics. But
Wedge was not a good Catholic. Hadn't she seen him with
her own eyes, eating meat on a Friday? Nor was he a good
son, to let Euphemia live in that rattrap when he possessed
ample means of getting her out of it. The man was fully capable of murdering his parent! If Neddy, a mere child, made
no distinction between his mother and the rest of the world,
then why should Wedge?

But just because he *could* have done it didn't mean that he
had. So what had actually happened? Arabella opened the
blue notebook and wrote:

Possible Chain of Events for O.W.

1. *offers to publish*
2. *overspends*
3. *is double-crossed*
4. *commits murder*

It made sense. Having arranged with Euphemia to publish her memoirs, Wedge had spent lavishly, anticipating huge dividends: a Thomas Lawrence portrait, beautiful clothes, Waterford crystal, and a bigger office at a more fashionable address. But Euphemia had double-crossed him by sending a circular letter to the would-be victims, pledging to destroy her notes on their peculiar personal habits in return for cash. When Wedge discovered how he'd been duped, he had hired a sailor to steal Arabella's paper knife, and then used it to murder Euphemia.

But how had Arabella come into it? Why would Wedge hire someone to steal *her* knife, having never met her?

She stared, unseeing, at the denture on the desk in front of her. At the denture. The denture that . . . Arabella grabbed Euphemia's open ledger: "gold plate—fraudd venturs—alley." And then, as if a veil had lifted and floated away from her eyes, she saw: "Gold plate—for adventures—Ollie."

Of course! Wedge had given his gold denture plate to Euphemia as an advance on the memoirs! He . . . went to her room for the manuscript, and she . . . had nothing to give him. She had already spent all her blackmail takings—on gambling, on drink, who knows? Euphemia had a talent for wasting money. So she had made up a dummy manuscript, probably. Tied up some bills or something in brown paper and handed it over. She must have! Because he had given her those teeth. The same teeth he was wearing when Tom Lawrence painted his portrait. The portrait that was still wet when Arabella had been in his office two weeks ago! By the time she had met Oliver Wedge, he was wearing another set, made by somebody else. *That* was why he had looked different in the portrait: His teeth had been larger, with a gap between the front ones.

Wedge had sworn to her that he had never seen the memoirs. Well, that had been true, because it had never been written. But he had also said he hadn't seen Euphemia since February. And that had been flatly contradicted by the dental plate's presence in the elephant box. Oliver Wedge had been lying through his teeth.

Chapter 16

A MAN OF HIS TIME

*Revelations and illuminations, in which Mrs.
Molyneux brings home the butter, Arabella goes
fishing, Mr. Kendrick comes through, and a
cunning plan is divulged.*

"Mrs. Janks," said Arabella, coming into the kitchen.
"Have we still got the newspapers from two
weeks ago?"

"Yes, my dear, some of them," replied the housekeeper,
pulling her spectacles down her nose. (She had been trying to
read a receipt book of Mrs. Moly's, but the French was beyond her.) "They're on the lower shelf in the pantry, left-
hand side. But they aren't all there; I use 'em as I needs 'em,
for wrapping fish scraps, an' that."

"Mmm! Fish! How good that sounds! But you . . . don't
have them *all,* Mrs. Janks?"

"Not there I don't. But if this has anything to do with your
murder case . . ."

"It has everything to do with it!"

"Well, I've saved clippings for you, miss, from all the papers as ever wrote about it, since the first day. They're up in
my room, pasted in an album."

"Oh, Charlotte!" cried Arabella, giving her an affectionate
squeeze. "You *are* a wonder! May I see them tonight?"

"Whenever you wants 'em, miss, they'll be there for you. I put the word out to all the servants in all the houses as I know, to save them articles for me."

"Do you have *The Tattle-Tale*'s, too?"

Mrs. Janks made a face. "Yes, miss. Even them ones."

"You," said Arabella, "are quite simply *the* most indispensable housekeeper in London, and I am doubling your salary, as of today."

As Mrs. Janks began to protest this, for form's sake, someone could be heard fumbling with a key at the service entrance. A moment later, Cook entered the kitchen with her market basket and plumped it on the table.

" 'Allo, Meez Beaumont," she said. "I 'ave brought beautiful lemons from ze market, and ze freshest buttair we 'ave evair ad!"

"Ooh!" cried Arabella excitedly. "And fresh fish, too, I'll be bound!"

"*Non!*" replied the cook. "Zee feeshing boats 'ave not come in. A zquall at sea 'as kept zem far out. Deed you feel like feeshing, yourself, mademoiselle?"

"Hmm, I suppose I could do. In fact, that is a capital idea, Mrs. Moly! I have a sudden fancy for fresh fish!"

But she was checked in the act of retrieving her rod and creel from behind the kitchen door by a loud wolf whistle issuing from Fisto's cage.

"The gardener's boy has arrived, ma'am," said the parlor maid, opening the door from the corridor. Over Fielding's shoulder, Arabella could see the young rajah, unhooking Fisto's cage.

"There you are, Moses! Let us go up to the breakfast room. I have taught Fisto a new verse for today. The prompt is 'La Ribbon Hat.' "

". . . is terribly fat," Fisto chanted, as they all went upstairs.

"And she scarcely has any bone.
So don't give her that chair,
As fragile as air,
For she weighs at least seventeen stone!"

Moses grinned. "I reckon that bird's as keen a pattering slang cove as ever came out of a toffkin, ain't he, miss?"

"Er, yesss . . . ," said Arabella. "But not half so keen a patterer as *I* am, you know, for it was me thought up the verses and taught him to say them."

". . . And *you're* not half so clever as Casanova was," said Belinda, entering the morning room with a basket full of lupines. "For *he* was the one who had this idea in the first place! Besides," she added, arranging the flowers in a tall vase, "Lady Ribbonhat is *not* fat. She looks something like a raisin."

"I know, but such women never feel thin enough. Just hearing someone say that she is big makes her worry that she might be."

"Well, but seventeen stone? That is so outrageous even *she* won't believe it."

"I had to use 'seventeen,' or the verse wouldn't have scanned. Besides, have you ever really looked at her head? It's enormous! I figure that her head weighs twelve stone all by itself, and then, we'll figure in another five, for the rest of her . . . that comes out to seventeen. Anyway, I can't stop to gossip now; I must go out and catch dinner."

One of the nicest things about Lustings was the stream meandering through its 2.5 acres. Not only was it picturesque—the Beaumont sisters and their artist friends often painted the views to be had from its banks—but it also contained succulent fish, which delighted in the rushing eddies and shady pools and often stopped here on their way downstream.

There was nothing Arabella loved more than to come outside by herself in the summer and think solitary thoughts whilst she angled. On this occasion, she had removed her shoes, propped up her pole within easy reach on an x-shaped block designed for the purpose, and leaned her back against a tree whilst simultaneously smoking a cigar and reading a book.

"Miss Beaumont? Miss Beaumont, are you somewhere hereabouts?"

"Damn!" muttered Arabella, shutting the book and laying aside her cigar. "Yes, Mr. Kendrick! Over here!"

The rector fought his way through the shrubs and bracken, to arrive at last, panting, by her side.

"Do you think it wise to be out in the sun?" he asked her, brushing himself off. "You'll go brown, you know, if you aren't careful."

"But I *am* careful; I have a large hat on, as you see, and I am sitting in the shade."

"Pray, do not let me interrupt you; we can talk whilst you fish."

"Have you ever fished, Mr. Kendrick?"

"No, as a matter of fact. I don't believe I have."

"I guessed as much. Fish will not bite during conversations, for they are shy creatures, and highly temperamental. If one should make a noise, or move about, they scatter and hide."

"Oh, yes?" said Kendrick. His mind being preoccupied with other matters—for he had noticed Arabella's shoes lying next to the cigar and was furtively admiring her attractive bare feet—the import took some time to sink in, and she waited for the light of comprehension to dawn upon his features.

"Oh! Oh, I say! I *am* sorry for having interrupted you, Miss Beaumont!"

"That is quite all right, Mr. Kendrick; your assistance with this case means more to me than all the trout in the world. I assume that is why you have come?"

"Yes, it is! . . . Er, does it really?"

"Indubitably."

She patted the grass beside her, and the rector unhesitatingly joined her there.

"Well," said she, "what have you discovered? I hope I have not sent you on a wild-goose chase?"

"On the contrary! I took your excellent drawing to Bond Street, where it was at once identified as the mark of Claudius Ash. I had only to cross the road and walk down a few doors to find the very man himself!"

"Well done, Mr. Kendrick! Your efficiency is admirable!"

"I am gratified that you think so, Miss Beaumont. Well, I recalled what you had said about discretion, so I told Mr. Ash that I was thinking of getting a denture made for my elderly mother. I said I heard that he had once made a splendid one for a Mr. . . . Mr. . . . 'Wedge,' he said. '*The Tattle-Tale* editor.' He came to the point very nicely, I thought."

"He did indeed!"

"I had expected that I would have to draw him out cunningly, but not a bit of it! The man would not *stop* talking! False teeth is a subject very near to his heart, it seems. He said that Wedge's plate was just a prototype—his only effort so far, but he thinks he has hit upon a good idea. Gold, you see, is soft—for a metal—and non-corrosive, so it may be more comfortably worn in the mouth than many other materials. He hopes to manufacture them one day. Ash has always been fascinated by what he termed 'the problem of teeth,' and when I made the mistake of complimenting him upon Wedge's plate, which I have not in fact seen, he launched into a description of the porcelain dentitions, and told me how he'd been able to make them so lifelike as to be indistinguishable from the real thing. He'd added a gap because Wedge had told him that his own teeth—which, by the way, were knocked out by a fellow he wronged—had had such a gap. I had a bit of a narrow squeak when Mr. Ash wanted to know all about my 'mother,' whether she needed upper and lower replacements or just an upper, because, he said, lower ones were more difficult to make and he hadn't ever done those before.

"But having already jeopardized my soul by telling one lie, I damned it entirely by telling another. I promised to bring the mater round and let him look inside her mouth, which I don't think I will, you know, as she died when I was seven. I can't suppose it would be very pleasant for poor Mr. Ash."

"Oh, that is capital!" cried Arabella delightedly. "You have done very well indeed, Mr. Kendrick!"

"Have I?" he asked, favoring her with a melting glance and lifting her hand to his lips. "I am . . . as always, your most devoted admirer, ma'am, and inexpressibly happy to have been of service to you."

"Then perhaps you would like to be in on the capture? I am now almost entirely certain that Oliver Wedge is our murderer."

"What, that scoundrel?" cried Kendrick. "I might have saved you a great deal of worry, then! If I had known that you suspected him, I should have named him at once as the culprit!"

"You would condemn a man without proof?"

"Such a man as he could not possibly be innocent!"

"It sounds as if you know him quite well."

"Not in the sense of being his 'chum,' if that's what you mean. But the man *is* known to me, and as you have already seen, he has made a decidedly ill impression!"

"But why?" asked Arabella. "What has he done?"

"He seduced my brother's fiancée, a sweet, innocent girl of seventeen summers, a girl so cloistered by her family as to think that babies were bought at the fair, like horses. She knew nothing of this wicked world, Miss Beaumont, nor of men, until she crossed paths with Oliver Wedge."

At this point, there was a sharp tug upon the fish line, and Arabella grabbed the pole, eventually landing a four-pound bream.

"I'm sorry, Mr. Kendrick," she said, rebaiting her hook. "Pray, continue. How did she meet Mr. Wedge?"

"Well," said he, "the unfortunate child had been keeping a diary throughout her courtship, filled with all her little maidenly hopes and feelings. It was her intention to present this book to her future groom as a gift, professionally printed and handsomely bound, and she had the great misfortune to take it to Wedge for that purpose.

"Her family always made sure that she was accompanied when out of doors by a chaperone. But a simple, elderly woman is no match for the devil! Wedge was easily able to separate the two females, and with the old one locked out, he effectively had his way with the young one in a back room."

"How like him!" sighed Arabella. "I mean," she said, rousing herself at Kendrick's expression, "that your story tallies exactly with my own impressions of the fellow. Then what happened?"

"My brother called him out, but Wedge ran away. Hayward chased the scoundrel through the streets, caught up with him at last, and knocked his teeth out. He hurt his own fist quite badly, too."

"And what of the girl?"

"How do you mean?"

"What happened to her?"

"Lord knows."

"What! Didn't your brother marry her, after all?"

"Of course not! He couldn't after . . . after Wedge had been there before him!"

"Oh, I see. It wasn't a love match, then."

"I don't know whether it was or not. I am not especially close with my brother. But I don't see that it signifies."

"Don't you, Mr. Kendrick? And yet, if I were to renounce my profession this minute, and swear never to have anything to do with it anymore, what would you say?"

"I should ask you to marry me."

"Have you any idea how many lovers I have had?"

"No! Nor do I want to know! I would ask only that I be the last."

"Yet your brother's fiancée had only had a *single* encounter. You seem to keep one set of standards for yourself, Mr. Kendrick, and quite another for the rest of the world. Tell me, if that unfortunate young woman had been *your* fiancée, would you still have married her?"

"I suppose so . . . yes, I believe I would have."

"And yet you never thought to censure your brother for his cruelty toward a blameless girl, who was ruined as the result of finding herself in a dangerous location with poor supervision? If that poor child can be blamed for anything at all, it is only of loving your brother enough to want to give him her diary."

The rector blushed.

"I am forced to admit that I had not thought of it in that light before," he said quietly. "Dear me, you are perfectly right, Miss Beaumont. I failed to do my duty to my brother, or to save that young girl from unjust blame and ignominy. I am deeply ashamed of myself."

"Well, you belong to the times in which you live, Mr. Kendrick, and escape is exceedingly difficult for any of us. But as long as you remain willing to examine your attitudes, and revise your opinions when necessary, I shall ever hold you in the highest esteem."

"Oh, Miss Beaumont! Do you hold me in high esteem? Do you, really?"

"Entirely, Mr. Kendrick," Arabella replied, handing him her second wriggling fish. "Now, here is what I am thinking: I shall hide you and the two Runners in my boudoir, and invite Mr. Wedge up to my bedroom. He will think, you know, that I am asking him up there to . . . but I must employ this ruse to be certain of his coming."

"Certain of his *what?*"

"Certain that he will accept my invitation."

"Oh."

"Do you not see the logic of it? If my plan incommodes you too much, I shall devise another, but that will take time, and he may leave town."

"Well," said the rector, gritting his teeth. "I think I had better hear your plan in its entirety before venturing an opinion."

"Thank you. At the right moment, I shall confront him. And when I am satisfied, . . . of his guilt, I mean, I shall call out to you and the others to come in and arrest him. What do you think?"

"I think it a very dangerous plan, Miss Beaumont. Perhaps you *should* try to invent another—one incurring less personal risk to yourself."

"But what risk could there possibly be, with you and the Runners right there in the next room? Really, Mr. Kendrick. Sometimes you act like a mother hen!"

"Where your safety is involved, I feel I cannot be too cautious. You can have no conception, Miss Beaumont, of what I would suffer if you should ever be harmed."

"I think I might have an inkling."

"Can you tell me why *you* suspect Wedge?"

"Well, at first I did not think he could have done it, once I learnt that Euphemia Ramsey was his mother."

"What!"

"Fantastic, is it not? Yet it is true; I have seen the proof. And in the social circles in which you and I are accustomed to spin, Mr. Kendrick, people do not murder their mothers. In other orbits, however, they are evidently less particular.

"Once I was disabused of my prejudice, I realized that Mr. Wedge must have left his gold dental plate with Euphemia as security for the memoirs. But of course, she didn't *have* the memoirs, had in fact never written them, as nearly all her victims had bought their way out in advance. I am guessing that she gave him something in return, however—perhaps a parcel of unpaid bills, wrapped in brown paper and tied with string—knowing that he wouldn't open it until he got back to his office.

"Imagine his thoughts when he discovered he'd been duped: 'That duplicitous cow!' (If one could conceive of such an animal, Mr. Kendrick.) 'She has spent the advance and taken my teeth, giving me nothing in return! I shall kill her!' And then he realizes that the sensational story of her murder will sell newspapers, so he writes up the article *before* committing the crime, to make sure that his version is the first to hit the streets. I must check this, but I am fairly certain that *The Tattle-Tale* account will be found to contain details of the murder to which no other papers were privy at the time.

"Finally, there is the problem of his being caught. He won't be, of course, if the crime can be blamed on someone else. 'On whom can I blame it, though?' he wonders. 'Whom did she hate?' Me, of course. I'm told that Euphemia was in the habit of cursing my name several times a day. 'If I frame this Arabella Beaumont,' thinks Wedge, 'I can run serialized special editions about the wicked lives of the two courtesans. I shall get Miss Beaumont to tell me her life's story, including the history of their feud. Then I shall cover the trial and visit her in prison, for the exclusive story of her final thoughts on the eve of her execution. I shall also, of course, cover the execution itself in detail, with a carefully observed description of her death throes at the end of the rope. Then, finally, I shall write a glorious book about the whole thing, from start to finish, based upon the articles I have written. From all these ventures I shall earn a fortune, and set myself up as a gentleman, at last!'

"That is what I think happened," said Arabella. "But of course, I cannot know for certain, until I ask Mr. Wedge."

Chapter 17

WHAT A SWEET PLACE YOU HAVE

*A seductive setting, a promising prelude,
and an unpleasant surprise.*

Arabella's bedchamber was sentimentally adorned with fat little candles and sweet-smelling flowers from the garden, so that it more resembled a grotto or a forest bower than an upstairs room in a private house. And Doyle had turned down the bedclothes and strewn rose petals between the sheets, before setting out a decanter of cherry brandy and two Venetian crystal glasses.

"By heaven, what a sweet place you have here," murmured Oliver Wedge, looking about him appreciatively. He sat upon her bed and poured out the brandy, handing one glass to Arabella and raising the other to her in silent tribute.

She sat beside him, and man and woman smiled at one another in the semi-darkness. Neither spoke. They took small sips, unconsciously synchronizing their breathing, whilst the throb of cricket song washed over them through the open windows.

At length, Oliver took Arabella's empty glass and set it down upon the tray beside his own. When he turned toward her, easing the gown from her shoulders, Arabella suddenly found she had no strength in her neck; the muscles seemed to dissolve, and her head fell back, as he planted hot kisses on her mouth, her throat, and her exposed breasts.

"All of you," he whispered in her ear. "I want to see all of you!" She remembered the remark he'd made when introducing himself: "Have you seen all of her, Wedge?" and realized that he had probably said this to every woman with whom he had ever enjoyed intimate relations. But that scarcely mattered, now. She allowed him to remove her gown. Arabella seldom wore a chemise, obscuring, as it did, the finer points of her figure. Nor did such ineffectual garments offer protection from wandering hands or thwart eager and unlawful glances. Her gown had in fact been all she was wearing, and now she wore it no longer.

"Turnabout is fair play, Mr. Wedge," she said, tugging at his shirt. And he obligingly removed everything *but* that article. She lay back on the bed. He knelt between her knees, his body levered over hers, when she said softly, "Darling, would you oblige me . . . by wearing something?"

He smiled above her in the darkness. "To give you pleasure is my one and only wish."

Arabella half-turned under him and pulled open the drawer of her nightstand. The duke's pistol lay there, sullen and murderous in the candlelight, but her hand fluttered over it and pulled out instead a set of very realistic porcelain teeth, affixed to a palate of gold.

"If you would be good enough," she said, handing it to him. "I should like you to take out your teeth and try these instead."

Wedge froze, and his eyes slid to meet hers in a moment of naked recognition.

"You killed Euphemia," she whispered. "Didn't you."

It was a statement, not a question.

His shocked glance hardened to a glare of piercing resolve, and he should have pierced her indeed had he still had her paper knife. This was the confirmation she wanted, and Arabella opened her mouth to call the men in from the boudoir. But swift and deadly as a barn owl grasping a mouse in its talons, Wedge seized her by the throat. And she was unable either to breathe or to mobilize her vocal cords to produce a single sound.

Chapter 18

THE ELEPHANT IS A NOISY CREATURE

*In which an act of desperation ultimately proves
fortuitous, Mr. Kendrick takes part in a
cover-up, and the criminal asks a favor.*

Arabella struggled for breath, twisting her neck in Wedge's grip as she tried to break free and clawing frantically at his wrist with both hands. But the reader will doubtless feel no surprise to learn that her efforts were wasted. Wedge was using only one hand—he was leaning on the other and seemed not even to be trying very hard—but Arabella was completely incapable of breaking his grip.

In the general course of polite day-to-day interactions between the genders, women seldom have cause to be conscious of men's superior strength. They know that this is so, accept it as an article of faith, but with the sad exception of abused wives and lovers, rarely experience it firsthand. Because when a man genuinely wishes to overpower a woman physically—unless he is ill or dying and she is an Amazon—there is no contest. The difference in physical strength between the sexes is enormous and unfair. A woman like Arabella can struggle with all her might against a man like Wedge and accomplish nothing. Which is doubtless why Nature, in the interests of evening the odds, has arranged for women to have superior *mental* strength that outstrips men's to an equal degree.

Now, as Arabella struggled in Oliver Wedge's stranglehold, she thought fleetingly of the pistol, theoretically so near yet in reality so distant. For though it lay mere inches from her head, getting it into her hand would have required her to shove off her attacker, turn over onto her left side, pull open the drawer, pull out the gun, ask him how to clean it, do so, ask for directions on reloading, accomplish that, and then aim it at him, with a fair amount of accuracy.

Almost as near and equally as inaccessible, John Kendrick and the two Bow Street Runners stood quietly waiting on the other side of the door, listening for Arabella's call. In time, they would doubtless sense something amiss and burst open the door without her summons, only to find her lying dead and Wedge escaped out the window.

All this flashed through her mind as she thrashed about in a panic, completely unable to breathe and beginning to black out, when in the corner of her eye she caught the gleam of candlelight on deep-red glass. Her elephant stood upon the nightstand, a silent witness to her last moments.

With all the strength that remained to her, Arabella flung out an arm, hitting the elephant broadside and smashing it against the wall with the explosive report that only five pounds of solid glass can produce. Wedge, startled, relaxed his grip for a moment, and as Arabella drew in a life-prolonging gulp of air the door of the boudoir burst open, admitting Kendrick and the constables into the room. A few moments later, the servants ran in, too, with lamps, and the darkened room was suddenly bathed in light. Wedge was manacled after a brief struggle, and Kendrick ran to Arabella, who was lying exposed upon the bed without so much as a ribbon to cover her nakedness. He yanked the coverlet from beneath her feet and cast it over her, before shifting her gently up and onto the pillows.

"Arabella," he cried. "Can you hear me? Arabella! Say something!" She began to cough, putting her hands up to her throat. "Quickly!" he barked at Doyle. "Bring water for your mistress, and fetch Miss Belinda!"

"She isn't here," Arabella rasped. "She's with the princess."

"I shall send someone to fetch her directly," said Kendrick. "Pray, do not try to talk, Miss Beaumont; water will be brought you shortly." And he poured out a glass of cherry brandy, to tide her over while she waited for the water.

The Runners, meanwhile, were helping Wedge get his breeches back on—a thing that is impossible to do alone with one's hands manacled behind one's back. Once they had made him presentable, he looked over at Arabella.

"You clever little vixen," he said admiringly. "Figured it all out and saved yourself, too, didn't you? My heartiest congratulations! I wonder if I might ask you a favor?"

"A favor, sir?" said Kendrick. "A *favor?!* You just tried to kill this woman! Take him away, officers!"

"No, wait," croaked Arabella. "What do you want, Mr. Wedge?"

"My teeth. They're the most comfortable set I own, and from what I've heard, prison is a most *un*comfortable place."

"Give them to him, would you, John?" she whispered. "Mr. Wedge, did you ever discover who vandalized your office?"

He smiled affably, as though the two of them were sitting on a pleasant terrace having tea.

"As a matter of fact, I did it myself," he said. "I had just published a scathing article about you, and I knew you would be stopping by before long to have it out with me. Do you remember what happened after you arrived, brimming with indignation and finding my place a shambles?"

Arabella looked at him.

"We had sexual congress on top of my desk. You see, madam, the successful womanizer knows how to set up the type of scenarios which are generally favorable to his success, and then exploit the results to his own advantage. Emotional, situational, and seasonal factors—everything plays a part, and all must be brought together with a light but steady hand."

Mr. Kendrick shut his eyes and massaged his temples, as though he had a headache. The Runners were blushing.

"I see," said Arabella hoarsely. "Thank you."

"No, Miss Beaumont, thank *you!*"

"When did you first decide to murder Euphemia?" she whispered. "Was it a slow process, or was there a single instant when you suddenly knew that you were going to kill her?"

"The latter," he said. "I made an instantaneous decision when I learned how the bitch had cheated me."

"Yes," said Arabella softly. "And did she give you a pile of trash, tied up like a manuscript?"

"No, she told me what she had done."

"Oh!"

"She admitted everything: how she had spent the advance, blackmailed her subjects, and taken my teeth as a further surety—she had let me read some of her notes before she'd torn them up, you see—but even then, as furious as I was, I had no thought of killing her. I asked her to give me my denture back, at least. But she refused."

Arabella nodded. "Euphemia never *did* give things back."

"I was just on the point of leaving then, with some vague idea of seeking legal redress, when she leered at me and said, 'Don't worry, Ollie; I've left in the bit about my relationship to *you*.' I didn't want that to get out; I had hopes of one day running for Parliament. But I told *you* about it, because I knew that you suspected me, and wouldn't, once you found out that I was her son."

"But—"

"I know. Ridiculous, wasn't it? The memoirs could never have been published, with so few pages. My secret was actually quite safe. It was the way she said it, I suppose. Her voice dripping with malice, a sneering sort of contempt. It infuriated me, but I understood it completely, because I'm just like that myself."

"Come along," said Constable Hacker. "There's other people wants to talk to you, my lad!"

"Adieu, Miss Beaumont," said Oliver Wedge. "I would kiss your hand, but I'm afraid that gesture is beyond me, bound as I am. We shall probably see one another at my trial, and please feel free to attend the execution, too. It should be quite festive."

Chapter 19

ON THE INTERDEPENDENCE OF THINGS

*In which Oliver Wedge is "banged out," Belinda
waxes philosophical, Arabella is almost boring, and
Lady Ribbonhat is vanquished, for the time being.*

On the following day, Arabella received a note informing her that Oliver Wedge had bequeathed her his portrait. "I should fetch it as soon as possible," he advised her, "before the creditors sweep in and carry everything off."

She sat and considered a moment. Did she even want the picture? A painting of the villain who had tried to kill her? She decided that she did. For he was also the one man, out of the multitudes she had known, who had come nearest to winning her . . . not love, exactly, but devoted admiration.

"I *do* want his portrait," she told Belinda. "And I am beyond words touched that he should want me to have it."

She went out to Fleet Street in person to fetch it, and two nice young apprentices took it down off the wall for her. As they passed through the office, carrying it between them, the rest of the staff all stood at attention, watching the image of their chief leave the premises forever. One man began to belabor the surface of a desk with his open hand. Another hit a press, as a third began to stamp upon the floor, and so on, until the room resounded with the thumping and clattering of wood being struck, with fists, with shoes, with pencil cups, anything.

It was the custom, Arabella knew, to bang an editor out as he exited his office for the last time, and Oliver Wedge, one of the portrait carriers explained, whatever else he may have been, was a first-rate newspaperman.

Everything was winding down now. Arabella had sent Moses out with Fisto for one last day, the bird having learnt his third verse:

> Lady Ribbonhat's friends have got over their hurts.
> To her ugliness they are inured;
> But the stench emanating from under her skirts
> Absolutely cannot be endured!

She had kept Fisto at home after that and sent a message to her foe:

> *Madam: Consider yourself fortunate that this has happened during the summer months, when everyone who can is gone into more congenial climes. I must stay on here to clear my name, and obviously you yourself have remained to try to snatch my home away from me, but everyone else of consequence is away now. If you persist in making my life more difficult than it presently is, I shall attempt to sell my bird, once again, when everyone returns in the fall. And by then I shall have taught him an amusing variety of new verses.*

No further outrages had been perpetrated since Fisto's first day at the Royal Exchange—no animal carcasses, no death threats, no midnight excrement deliveries—nor were any anticipated. For Lady Ribbonhat must have guessed that Arabella had not yet begun to fight and was capable of much lewder poetry than she had heretofore devised. Discretion, as Constance would have said and as Lady Ribbonhat knew to her cost, was the petticoat of valor.

"Bell, do you remember, when we were at the auction, how you told me that you needed to have the red elephant in your life?"

The sisters were taking their customary constitutional, strolling arm in arm through Hyde Park, closely followed by their carriage, in case they should grow tired.

"Vaguely."

"Well, *I* remember. And now it has fulfilled its purpose. You had to get that elephant, and put it on your nightstand, so that you could break it on the floor and summon help when you needed it! Only think: If you had failed to outbid everyone else that day, you would be dead now."

"Hmmm."

"It only proves what I have long suspected: that we are mere puppets in a universe where every action, every thought we have, is pre-ordained. We are quite powerless either to prevent or to alter the course of events in any manner whatsoever."

" 'The Interdependence of Things,' " Arabella said.

Belinda groaned. "Not Lucretius, again!"

"No, indeed, Ernst Hoffmann, a well-known German critic and musical director, who occasionally writes stories. Although, I suppose, 'The Interdependence of Things' *could* be construed as a sort of codicil to *The Nature of Things*," she said, more to herself than to Belinda. "Similar titles, too. Herr Hoffmann has undoubtedly read Lucretius! I must write to him, and ask!"

"Bell," murmured her sister. "You're beginning to bore me."

If there was one thing upon which the Beaumont girls were in perfect agreement, it was the sin of not being fascinating.

"No, wait!" cried Arabella. "It's a story, you see—Euchar and his friend Lothair are walking through a park, even as we are now, on a summer's eve, exactly like this one, with a cool breeze that rises up to drive out the heat of the afternoon. The two are passing the picnickers—" here she broke off and nodded to Lord Carisbrooke, who was seated on the grass and eating tongue sandwiches with his family—"while making their way toward the pleasure gardens. . . ." (They could hear the strains of music drifting out from Vauxhall.) "And having this exact conversation. Euchar seems to have been expressing himself with regards to random chance, for Lothair, in the opening lines of the tale, passionately denies its existence. He compares the universe to a clock, crafted by a vast intelligence, and says that if chance were to interfere, everything would come to an immediate standstill. Then he trips over a root, and his friend laughingly tells him, if he had not tripped and fallen at that very moment, the universe would have vanished upon the instant."

"Oh," said Belinda. "And then what happens?"

"I don't know. Mr. Hoffmann hasn't finished the story yet. What I've told you was based on some notes he enclosed in a letter to Robert Southey. There's to be a Gypsy dancer in it."

At that moment, Belinda stumbled over a root and went sprawling upon the grass, to the vast delight of the onlookers.

"This," said Arabella, assisting her sister to rise and pulling her skirt down, "is a perfect example of the need for an all-enveloping garment that women can wear beneath their gowns, to shield their personal parts from the eyes of strangers."

Arabella felt nervous for Belinda, and with good reason; she had seen Tom Rowlandson sitting at some little distance away, sketch pad in hand. Odds were good, *very* good, that Belinda would find herself caricatured in Ackermann's window in the next day or two, sprawled upon the grass and completely exposed below the waist.

"Are you hurt, Bunny?"

"My dignity is bruised, and more than a little, but I believe I shall live," said the plucky girl. "Bell, do you suppose that by tumbling down just now, I saved the universe from exploding?"

"Oh, I don't know. It makes my stomach ache to talk about such things. Let us go home, and see whether Mrs. Moly has any of that chocolate sponge left over from luncheon."

Chapter 20

ALL'S WELL THAT ENDS. WELL . . .

*In which Mr. Kendrick ponders the future and
Arabella attempts to secure it.*

As he surmounted the steps to Lustings's front door, Mr.
Kendrick was surprised to see the two Runners still lurk-
ing about in the undergrowth.

"Oh, they're not here for *me*," Arabella explained. "They
have come to say good-bye to Neddy and Eddie. My niece
and nephew are returning to their respective homes today.
Do you know, the officers have grown quite close to those
children? Those poor, fatherless children!"

"But they're *not* fatherless! They're Charlie's!"

"It amounts to the same thing, does it not?"

"Are they really here to say good-bye to the children? Or
have they come to say hello to the mothers?"

"It amounts to the same thing, does it not?" she repeated.
"Speaking of that, Mr. Kendrick, I do not wish to appear
rude, but what have *you* come for? Are you taking up another subscription for those Effing Sunday school children?"

"No," he said, smiling. "This is purely a social call. I
wanted to be sure of catching you before you left for Bath."
Kendrick removed his hat and seated himself on one of the
large trunks in the foyer. "When do you go?"

"The day after tomorrow," said Arabella. "And I don't

mind telling you, Mr. Kendrick, that I cannot remember ever having needed a vacation so much in my life before!"

"I can well believe that. But have you given any thought to your future? Now that you have broken with the duke, you will need to find an alternative source of income, will you not?"

"I expect all will soon be sorted out to my satisfaction, in one way or another."

"That's very well for now," said Kendrick, "but what will you do when you're old?"

"I don't know," replied Arabella. "What do old people generally do?"

"They play with their grandchildren."

"I shall play with my friends instead. Other than that, I expect I shall behave much like other old ladies: I shall take naps. Spoil the dog. Crochet—as long as my eyes hold out."

"But you don't have a dog. And you have told me that you don't know how to crochet."

"It should be fairly easy to obtain a dog from somewhere. As to crocheting, I can always learn. And then at long last, when all my other interests have palled and I have nothing ahead of me but time, I shall work upon the crowning achievement of my life: my memoirs!"

Kendrick was flabbergasted.

"Oh! But. . . !"

Before he could formally protest, however, Fielding put her head through the doorway.

"The duke to see you, ma'am."

"Ah! Punctual to the dot! Put him in the library, Fielding. I shall send for him shortly."

The head was withdrawn.

"What do you mean?" Kendrick asked. "How is it the duke? Have you written to him?"

Arabella drew herself up with an air of injured dignity. "Of course not! For what do you take me, Mr. Kendrick?"

But her manner softened immediately. "I happen to know the date on which Miss van Diggle broke their engagement— she's called 'Jiggle van Diggle,' by the way. Suits her, don't you think?—and Glen*deen* is due to ship out on the twenty-ninth. So I have allowed him a day to shop for gifts to woo me back, and two more for his mother to threaten him with disinheritance if he takes up with me again. That brings us to today, the twenty-eighth. If we narrow it down still further, today is Friday, Puddles' day to play golf with the bishop. Then I simply add the time it takes for him to look in at his club and dine at Co's. Ordinarily, he *might* have gone to the opera, which would have added a few hours, but the duke has been abstaining from carnal pleasures these last few weeks, so on that account he will probably forego the opera and come straight to me. That puts his expected time of arrival here at about half past nine—"

Arabella turned to the clock on her mantel, which was chiming the half hour. "*Et voilà!* But for the fact that Glen-*deen* would have seen it, I'd have listed his estimated arrival time in the betting book at White's and made a packet. But no matter: With the duke back in my fold, I shall make a packet anyway."

She lifted her eyes to the reverend's and laid her hand upon his arm. "Please don't fret, John," she said gently. "If the choice were mine alone, I should choose your company over that of any man's in London . . . now. However, I have obligations just at present."

"Yes," he said, smiling. "And you're much obliged *for* those presents, I'll be bound!" He covered her hand with his own. "It grieves me to know that I cannot support you and your family in the style you deserve."

"I know it does. But there may well come a time when I can make do with less. Belinda may marry. Charles may, too, for the matter of that, and finally assume full financial responsibility for his children. Pigs might fly . . . anything might happen. But a life for you and me together just now is impossible."

"Miss Beaumont," he said, and it was nice of him to call her so. For he had, after all, recently seen her quite naked. A man of less refinement would have called her Arabella. "I know it's indelicate to bring up figures at a time like this, but . . . if I may ask . . . how much would you require . . . do you think. . . ."

Her silvery laugh held more than a hint of gold in it, too. "Money is always an appropriate subject, Mr. Kendrick, as far as I am concerned. These days I am getting along on something over one hundred thousand pounds a year."

The reverend swallowed. "Ah!" That was all he said. But after a moment, he added, "You know how I feel about you, Miss Beaumont. I only ask that you remember I am always at your service; and pray, feel free to call upon me whenever you require assistance."

So saying, he raised her hand to his lips and left her.

Later that evening, Arabella lay in bed, amidst a profusion of boxes and ribbons, playing delightedly with the presents that the duke had heaped upon her counterpane in dazzling profusion: amber earrings; a matching set of diamond bracelets; a large diamond and sapphire starburst brooch; tortoiseshell combs, inset with emeralds; cashmere shawls in varying shades of green; and a Cavalier King Charles spaniel puppy. The duke, who sat on the edge of the bed, pulling off his boots, smiled down indulgently at his own darling domestic pet.

"There, you see?" he said. "It's all come right in the end, hasn't it, Bell?"

"I suppose so," she replied, nuzzling her puppy, "but it was a near thing, Puddles, a very near thing indeed."

The puppy was also called Puddles. In choosing this appellation, Arabella had been motivated less from sentimental impulse than from the *aptness* of the name. For the dog had already spoilt Arabella's bedside rug and she had decided to give it away to Neddy—the dog, not the rug—as soon as the duke had sailed for Portugal.

"Nonsense!" He laughed. "I told you I would take care of everything. You must learn to *trust* me, Bell."

"Yes, Henry," she replied. "Before you leave me tomorrow, darling, would you oblige me by signing a document?"

"A document?"

"Oh, it isn't anything, really. Just a little codicil. In case you should meet with misfortune in Palermo, you know. I've got it all written up, and Constance and Belinda will meet us downstairs tomorrow morning to witness it. Then we shall have a hearty breakfast together, and I shall kiss you goodbye and wish you Godspeed."

The duke was in a splendid humor. Arabella's sense of timing in approaching him thus had been flawless, as always.

"What am I to leave you in this 'little codicil'?" he asked, chucking her under the chin. "You've already got Lustings out of me."

"Yes. But I want to know that I may keep my carriage and jewels, as well—even the ones which have been in your family since the Conquest. And . . . so that I won't ever have to sell anything off in order to live, the way poor Euphemia did, I think I should like a lifetime yearly stipend of something over . . . well, let us say . . . one hundred thousand pounds."

Please turn the page for an exciting sneak peek
of Pamela Christie's second
Arabella Beaumont mystery . . .
coming soon from Kensington Publishing!

ONE GOD; TWO HORNS

"Well," said Belinda, "I think he would look remarkably fearsome emerging from the shrubbery, all hard and excited. From that vantage point, anyone sitting in the pergola might imagine herself about to be ravished!"

"Perhaps," Arabella replied. "All the same, I believe I shall place him on a pedestal, in the center of the reflecting pool."

The Beaumont sisters were huddled over the desk in the library, admiring a sketch of a large bronze statue from the buried city of Herculaneum, which Arabella had recently purchased, sight unseen, from a dealer in plundered antiquities.

"The workmen will have to tunnel in, you see," she explained. "And the removal will be extremely dangerous, because of cave-ins and poisonous gas pockets. I expect that is why I am being charged so much for it."

"Well, for that; and for the extra bit."

They studied the picture again. Arabella, who always liked to examine certain features in the best possible light, was using the magnifier.

"Yes," she said. "I have seen hundreds, if not thousands, of statues depicting naked manhood, Bunny, but this is the first I have ever beheld with *two* manhoods."

"Hmm . . ." mused Belinda. "That short, slender one on

top, and then the longer, thicker one beneath it . . . Whatever must the sculptor have been thinking?"

"Oh, come now; you know very well what he was thinking! And once I install this piece in my garden, everyone else will be thinking it, too. Yes," she said with a sigh, "you are probably right; I expect I *am* being charged extra for the extra bit. And because the piece is so old," she added, "and extremely beautiful."

". . . and because you are rich," finished Belinda. "All the same, though, something about this does not feel quite right. Oughtn't the statue to stay in the ground, with its dead owner? I mean, it is a kind of memorial now, is it not?"

Arabella put down the magnifier. "I wish you would not be so morbid, Bunny. The owner may very well have escaped the cataclysm, you know, and died years later, in Tarraconensis or some place. Besides, this is *Pan!* Pan, in an amorous attitude! A *doubly* amorous attitude! Even if the owner *did* die when the house fell on him, what sort of memorial would that be?"

"I don't know—a memorial to the perpetually stiff, perhaps."

Peals of girlish laughter flowed out through the door and along the passage, where the peerless Doyle was headed upstairs with an arm full of freshly ironed flannel nightgowns, and the incomparable Fielding was toting a cord of wood to the drawing room fireplace. It was autumn, Arabella's favorite season, and the nights were chilly now. So were the days, for the matter of that, and the one currently drawing to its close had pulled a thick mist over Brompton Park like a new shroud; all-of-a-piece, without any holes, yet fitting so closely as to reveal the sharper angles of the trees and houses beneath it.

In the countryside, such mists are Mother Nature's diaphanous veils, like transitional curtains between this world and the next. Not in London, though. The rivers here form foul repositories for those substances which man flings away from him in disgust, and when the mist rises off the water, collecting to itself all the available moisture, this filthy residue is condensed and distilled into poison. Most Londoners are hardy enough to survive such miasmas, but even the fittest are often subject to chronic coughs and sick headaches in the autumn.

Arabella loved this season, nevertheless. The rich smell of the woods in Regent's Park gladdened her heart when she took her walks there, the flame-colored leaves bringing out the deep auburn tones of her hair. She enjoyed reading by the fire, with a quilt thrown over her legs, and bowls of hot negus enjoyed in the company of convivial persons. No sensation could compare with slipping between flannel sheets heated with the warming pan on a chilly night, and few events could so reliably elevate her spirits like donning a fur-lined, fur-trimmed pelisse before stepping into her carriage on her way to the theater.

Most of all, though, she loved what autumn did to men—the way it made them want to snuggle up next to some warm female body and reward the owner of said body for favors bestowed. Gentlemen of her acquaintance were apt to be especially generous in the autumn. The Duke of Glen*deen*, for example, her own particular protector when he wasn't off fighting naval battles, had just presented her with six magnificent horses of a most unusual color. Hides like golden toast they had, with black manes and tails. Three of them, anyway. The other three were cream-colored, but they, too, had the dark manes and tails. Arabella had started a regular trend in carriage horses with these beauties: three each of two complementary colors, as opposed to the more traditional, perfectly matched sets. The idea was very new and widely imitated. And all she had done was to murmur one morning, as she and the duke lay together after a particularly vigorous quarter of an hour, that her carriage horses were tiring more easily, now they were older. Puddles was always a generous patron—Arabella never wanted for anything—but *six* horses! And it wasn't even her birthday! Yes, she adored the autumn.

Belinda did, too. But then, Belinda loved all the seasons, as she loved the whole world, being by nature a happy, tender, appreciative creature. The poor child was a trifle morose this evening, however, for the capricious princess regent had abruptly terminated their friendship without giving a reason, and Arabella had shewn her sister the sketch of the naughty statue to cheer her up. It had worked for a few minutes, but now that Belinda had seen it, enjoyed a laugh over it and offered her opinion on where it should be placed, she was pensive again.

"I should be glad this has happened, I know; the woman is selfish and vulgar, and I am well rid of her."

"Yes, you are! Only consider," said Arabella, "what was the princess wearing, the last time that you saw her?"

"Oh! A profusion of colors, which jumped and clashed together like I-do-not-know-what, covered by an ill-fitting spencer of lilac satin! Her gown was cut so low that the tops of her nipples were exposed! I cannot recall the rest."

"Not even her shoes?"

"Oh, yes! Half-boots! Primrose-yellow ones, with the flesh of her fat legs hanging over the tops, and a cap like a pudding bag—with the pudding still in it!"

Belinda was giggling now.

"Wait a bit," cried Arabella. "Shakespeare has described that very thing!"

She opened *The Taming of the Shrew,* which she was reading for the fourth or fifth time, and leafed through it till she found Petruchio's scene with the haberdasher.

" 'A custard coffin!' she said triumphantly. "One would think the bard was describing modern apparel! How ever does he *do* that?"

But Belinda had grown listless again. "I was hoping that

the princess would introduce me to someone I might marry—
I do so hate being a burden on you, Bell!"

"You could not possibly be a burden, dear! You are a
wonderful, darling companion, and the longer you stay with
me, the better I shall be pleased."

"Truly? Oh, I am glad *somebody* wants my company. Because it *is* humiliating to be dropped, even by a person as
horrid as the Wolfen Buttock!"

(This was the Beaumonts' private nickname for the princess, whose title before her marriage was Caroline of
Brunswick-Wolfenbüttel.)

"Of course it is humiliating, Bunny. But you must try to
forget about it. Because Lord Carrington is on the brink of
proposing to you, and you need to look as pink-cheeked and
sparkling-eyed as you possibly can, for him."

Belinda smiled at this, and there stole across her countenance such an expression of dreamy contentment that it did
her sister's heart good to see it. But Bunny's heavenward gaze
was interrupted in its journey up the library wall by the portrait of Oliver Wedge which hung there, and her smile faded.

"Bell," she said. "I own I do not understand why you keep
that thing!"

Arabella regarded the picture with wistful affection.

"For three good reasons and one foolish one: as the last
bequest of a dying man, as a warning not to trust in surface
appearances, and as a reminder to believe in myself—to recall that I may, with application, accomplish miracles."

"With application . . . and *my* assistance, d'you mean?"

"Of course, Bunny! I should never have tried to save myself from the gallows, but for your urging!"

"And the fourth reason?"

Arabella rose and began to pace the room. "You have
just had the three good ones. Can you not be satisfied with
those?"

"No! I want the foolish one, as well!"

Arabella sighed with feigned reluctance—for, really, she was all eagerness to tell it. "Because," said she, stopping beneath the portrait and gazing up at it. "He was the best lover I have ever had, or am ever likely to have."

"Oh, Bell; how can you say so? With only one encounter, on an untidy desk top? It was probably just the danger that somebody might walk in upon you."

"Pooh! I should not have cared if they had! But there is something in what you say: the danger." She glanced out her window at the misty garden. "When . . . he was strangling me, I was certain I would die. But when he stopped, just for a moment, I felt . . . as though . . . I wanted to have his child."

Belinda was shocked to the core. "That is the most perverted statement I have ever heard you utter!"

"I know. As I said, it was only for a moment. The feeling passed. But the memory of the feeling haunts me still."

"Some people are addicted to danger," said Belinda. "They seek it out because it gives them a kind of thrill not otherwise obtainable. I truly hope that you are not one of those people—they have a tendency to die years before their time."

"Me? Heavens, Bunny; what nonsense! I am perfectly happy as I am. Home at Lustings, with my library and my cook, my trout stream, my parchment ponies and my aviatory. What more could I possibly want?"

"I'm sure *I* could not say, if *you* could not," said Belinda, with an injured air.

"I shall tell you, then," said Arabella, pulling her sister up from the chair and enfolding her in her arms. "The love and constant support of the best, the dearest little sister in all the world!"

Belinda, mollified, returned her embrace, glancing down over Arabella's shoulder at the sketch of the statue.

"Perhaps," she reflected, "we should place him in the aviatory."

"Oh, no, dear; he would be coated with droppings inside of a week!"

"Birds fly over the garden, too."

"Yes, but he stands more of a chance outside." Arabella picked up the letter and gazed at the little sketch with fond affection. "Now, why could not *this* have been the deity who created man in His own image?"

"Because," said Belinda, simply. "Life is not fair."

Chapter 2

A BAD BUSINESS

It was too late in the year for crickets, even in Italy. But a threatening storm lent the proper atmospherics as a knot of men stood waiting beside an excavation in the cold wind. Around them, the ghostly ruins of a dead city bore mute witness to their activities, and one of the company gave a nervous start as a palm frond rattled in the night air. All eyes were fixed upon the tunnel entrance.

"Here they come," said one of the men.

"Quiet!" hissed another.

(The reader may wonder at anyone hissing that word, since it contains no sibilants in English, but these men were speaking Italian, in which language I presume the word has an "s" in it.)

Dark lanterns were lifted as four members of the company emerged from the mouth of the tunnel, struggling and grunting with the effort of a heavy burden wrapped in rough sacking, borne amongst them. One of the men stumbled.

"Careful with that!" growled the fellow who seemed to be in charge. This might have been deduced from the thin piece of pressboard he carried, to which a large metal clip was attached and firmly clamped over a tablet of paper, for it is well-established that no other accessory conveys more authority to the mind of civilized man, except a row of medals on the breast of a uniform, or possibly, a crown.

Having set their bundle upright upon the ground, the men proceeded to pad it with more sacking, followed by a layer of canvas and a girdle of ropes. Then they wrestled it onto a small donkey cart standing ready nearby, to which other similarly wrapped items had already been consigned.

"That's the last of them," said the fellow with the clipboard. "Now, let's get clear of this place before . . ."

But the man's remark, like his life, was suddenly cut short by a shovel, the assailant coming down from behind with such force that the back of the victim's skull was cleft nearly in twain. At the same moment, an earsplitting thunderclap broke directly overhead, followed immediately by a torrential downpour, which drenched the men to the skin. One of their number leapt into the cart and drove it off as the others seized their tools and melted into the darkness.